The Fetti Girls 2

Lock Down Publications & Ca$h Presents
The Fetti Girls 2
By
Destiny Skai

The Fetti Girls 2

Lock Down Publications
P.O. Box 1482
Pine Lake, Ga 30072-1482

Visit our website at **www.lockdownpublications.com**

Copyright 2017 The Fetti Girls 2

First Edition September 2017
Printed in the United States of America
This is a work of fiction. Names, characters, places, and incidents either are products of the author's imagination or are used fictitiously. Any similarity to actual events or locales or persons, living or dead, is entirely coincidental.

Cover design and layout by: Dynasty's Cover Me
Book interior design by: Shawn Walker
Edited by: Lauren Burton

Destiny Skai

Stay Connected with Us!

Text **LOCKDOWN** to 22828 to stay up-to-date with new releases, sneak peaks, contests and more…
Thank you!

Submission Guideline

Submit the first three chapters of your completed manuscript to ldpsubmissions@gmail.com, subject line: Your book's title. The manuscript must be in a .doc file and sent as an attachment. Document should be in Times New Roman, double spaced and in size 12 font. Also, provide your synopsis and full contact information. If sending multiple submissions, they must each be in a separate email.

Have a story but no way to send it electronically? You can still submit to LDP/Ca$h Presents. Send in the first three chapters, written or typed, of your completed manuscript to:

LDP: Submissions Dept
Po Box 1482
Pine Lake, Ga 30072

DO NOT send original manuscript. Must be a duplicate.

Provide your synopsis and a cover letter containing your full contact information.

Thanks for considering LDP and Ca$h Presents.

Acknowledgements

First and foremost I would like to thank God for giving me the ability to finish out my dreams. I've been down a rough path but with His grace and mercy, I was able to turn that negative into something positive. Secondly, my kids, Torrence and Ethan, without them I wouldn't go as hard as I do. I'm doing this for my young kings. My mom and dad, Denise Thomas and Robert McNeal, thank you for keeping me in prayer.

Now that I've gotten the formal introduction out of the way, I can get to it now. My family means the world to me and without their love and support, I wouldn't be in the position that I'm in now. There are too many of us to name, but my family is beyond PETTY and if I don't mention some of their names I will never hear the end of it. So, I would like to give a HUGE shot out to my Parkway, 6th court family: Xernora, Tayana, Sonya, Fannie, Genise, Sabrina H. Quontrail and my favorite boo/hustler, Yushika Brown.

A special thanks goes to my driving partner/my favorite dude El' Hefe aka Germ. I really appreciate you for taking the time to drive me to Atlanta for my very first event: The Atlanta Kickback. Without you and your mom, Sonya, that would've never been possible for me and I love y'all for that. I am FOREVER GRATEFUL. And because of that I was able to meet my favorite girl from Texas.

Helene Young, words cannot express the way I feel or the love I have for you. It meant so much to me when you showed up with *THE FETTI GIRLS* dressed up and representin' my book on y'all shirts. That made a QUEEN feel very special.

My LDP family, thank you for your continued love and support through my journey to success.

Shawn Walker, you've been nothing but helpful to me. From teaching me the correct format of a story, showing and not telling, all the way down to doing interview questions (that we haven't finished). Although you told the BOSS about Black Chyna (insider) I still love you.

And last, but certainly not least, the man of the hour, my mentor, my headache and BOSS, KING CA$H. I respect you as a businessman and a friend. You have coached me since the day I signed with you and stayed on me, even when I wanted to quit after I received my very first edits. Lol!! Thank you for believing in me.

Thank you to every person that has supported me from the very beginning, up until now. I am grateful for all of you. Follow me on all social media sites: author destiny skai. And also, if you have not read the series BRIDE OF A HUSTLA, make sure you check that out, as well as the movie that was released on July 30, 2017. Bride of Hustla, the movie, is now available for purchase on DVD. Inbox me for details.

Love Always,
Destiny Skai

Destiny Skai

Prologue

Chyna sat up on the sofa. "Hey, B, we're thinking about selling the house and moving further north so we can be low-key. Fuck out west."

That caught me off guard. "Like out of town north?"

"Nah," she laughed. "Palm Beach north."

I was relieved to hear that. "Okay, that's cool. This house is a little too hot, and ain't no telling who else she told."

"That's true," Mercedes added. "It's time for a new start, anyway. You and Corey getting married, so it's time for us to do our own thing."

I got up from the couch. "We should go out for lunch and have a few drinks."

Sierra finally opened her mouth and put her phone down. "I'm with that."

"Girl, bye," I laughed. "Your brother not about to kill me."

"I can't wait until I turn 18," Sierra pouted.

"Girl, the drinking age is 21. See, that's why you can't drink now: you don't know the law," Chyna teased her.

They all got up off the sofa and went outside. I pulled my keys out and walked toward my car. "I'll drive."

"Wait, Barbee, I left my phone," Sierra shouted. "Mercedes, can you open the door for me, please?"

While Mercedes let Sierra in, Chyna and I stood outside the car, talking. Suddenly, our conversation was cut short by a loud noise. When I looked toward the road, I saw a black van with men hanging out. Then I came to the realization the noise was a gunshot.

I grabbed my Glock from under the seat and let off a few rounds. All I could hear were gunshots and screaming. My mind was racing, and instantly I thought about Sierra. I was certain those were her cries. I knew I needed to protect her the same way Corey would. He would never forgive me if anything happened to his sister on my watch.

Crouching down behind my car, I looked toward the door because Mercedes was no longer in my eyesight. The gunfire felt as if it lasted for hours, and the ground was hot as hell. I needed to get up, but I was out of ammo. Something told me to crawl to the back of the car, and when I did I saw Chyna lying on the ground, covered in blood.

"Chyna!" I screamed from the top of my lungs. I immediately jumped up and rushed to my sister's aid. Nothing else around me mattered at that moment, not even the gunmen who were still shooting. I knelt down and tried to pick her up, but I could feel something pierce my back, and it felt hot, but I ignored it. However, I heard the screeching of the tires as they fled the scene.

"Please don't leave me, Chyna. Keep your eyes open."

She smiled. "I'm tired, Bee. I love you."

"No, Chyna, keep them open."

"I'm trying to, but I'm sleepy."

I could hear more screams behind me, but they sounded muffled.

"Barbee, I called the police and Corey. They're on the way," Sierra panicked.

The next thing I knew, I collapsed, and I could feel Sierra lifting up my body. She placed my head in her lap, and I could hear her cries.

"Barbee, please don't leave us. Corey needs you, and so do I. We love you. Please, don't go."

I felt a single teardrop fall into my eye from hers before I closed mine.

Chapter 1

Barbee

The past two months were extremely rough for Corey, but he was getting through it slowly with the help of Sierra. Mentally he had come a long way, and he couldn't have done it without her. He walked slowly down the row, through the freshly-cut grass of the cemetery with his head down. This was his third trip in one week.

Stopping in front of the headstone, he sat the flowers in the vase. Despite the nature of the visit, the weather was perfect, which made it easier to sit for a long period of time. The sun was playing hide and seek behind the clouds. The wind was cool, as if winter was around the corner.

Corey sat down on the grass and looked to his right, thinking about the way life works. Anyone could be here today and gone tomorrow. Life was too short to take for granted, and it was important for everyone to tell the ones they love that they love them because no one will ever know when it's their last day.

"Are you okay?" he asked.

I shook my head no. "I'll never be okay."

He put his arm around me, and I rested my head on his chest. "Yes, you will, and I'm going to make sure of that."

"I can't believe she's gone," I sobbed loudly. "That was my sister and my best friend."

Corey sat quietly and listened to me vent.

"And what about our unborn child? What if I can't give you another baby?"

"Babe, stop beating yourself up about this. I'm hurt too, but at the end of the day all I'm worried about is you. If it's in God's will, we will get pregnant again. If not, we can always adopt. I love you, and I'm not leaving you for nothing in this world."

The day I was shot, the doctor told Corey I was pregnant and the bullet struck and killed the baby. I had a lot of internal bleeding, but they were able to stop it and save me with the help of surgery. On the scene I lost consciousness, and they thought I was going to die. What hurt the most was after I woke up, I found out Chyna was dead. I wanted to die right along with her, so they kept me under suicide watch. Then I found out about the baby, and that made it worse because I never knew I was pregnant in the first place. I questioned God about why he took my child away. Then I remembered I didn't want to have kids, so maybe that was my punishment.

Since Chyna had been gone, I had completely given up on life. I didn't get my hair done, put on clothes, or step foot out of the house. The only time I came out was when I would come to visit Chyna for hours at a time. Corey tried to motivate me and give words of encouragement, but it wasn't working. Regardless of that fact, I was happy to have him by my side. He was what I needed to keep me alive.

The more I thought about it, the angrier I got. "Ugh!" I screamed. "I just wanna kill that muthafucka."

"No. I can't afford to lose you like that. Let me and Amon handle this. I need you to get better."

I dropped my head.

"Listen to me, Barbee. I almost lost you once. I refuse to let you put yourself in danger. How many times do I have to say I love and need you here with me?"

The drive back to the house was a silent one. All I could do was look out the window and cry. Once we were home, I went to bed. Sleeping the days away had become a normal routine for me. I cried myself to sleep with Corey next to me. Every so often I would jump out of my sleep, drenched in sweat because all I could hear were gunshots and screaming. When Corey had to leave, Sierra would take his place and lay with me. Every day the pain felt more severe than the day before, and that's because in the hospital I was feeling my very own pain from the gunshot. Now that I was back home, mourning the loss of my sister and unborn child. I knew my life would never be the same.

When I awoke from a very long nap, I could hear laughter coming from the living room. I didn't bother going out there because I wasn't feeling sociable, so I just lay there going through my phone, looking at pictures of me and Chyna. After a while it became too much to bear, and I threw it against the wall and pulled the covers over my head. Seconds' later I heard the bedroom door open, but I didn't bother to look.

Corey pulled the blanket from over my head. "What was that noise? Are you okay?"

"It was my phone."

He picked it up off the floor. "Why did you throw your phone?"

"I was looking at pictures of me and Chyna," I admitted.

Corey grabbed my arm. "Get up." He was quite demanding. "I can't let you do this to yourself. It's been two months, and it's time to move on with your life."

I was a little pissed with his bluntness, but I didn't say anything.

"I know you're hurting, but doing this to yourself is not going to bring her back. You lost your sister, but your mother lost her daughter, someone she gave birth to, and she's not acting like this."

"Leave me alone and let me die already."

"Listen to you." He shook his head. "I know Chyna is disappointed in you right now. This is not like you, and I'm not letting you stay in bed another day." He pulled me up to my feet. "You need to go shower and put on some clothes. We're getting out of the house."

It took a little over and hour for me to get dressed. Sierra tried to help me, but Corey stopped her, saying something about being an enabler. He grabbed his keys.

"Let's go."

"Where are we going?" I asked.

"We're going out." Sierra was smiling. "It's going to be fun."

Twenty minutes into the car ride, I was getting aggravated. "Where are we going?" I asked again, but this time with annoyance in my voice. Corey wasn't fazed, as usual.

"We're almost there." he assured me.

Shortly after that we pulled up to a building that had a lot of cars outside. I looked around to see where the hell I was. "Did you bring me to a club, Corey?"

"We're not staying. I just need a few minutes to speak with the owner," he replied.

"For what?" I folded my arms across my chest.

"Sierra's birthday party. Y'all come on."

I was hesitant at getting out, but Sierra seemed excited and I didn't want to ruin it for her just because I didn't want to enjoy life. As we walked up to the door, there was a sign up, but it was covered.

I held Corey's hand tight so I wouldn't fall. "It's so dark in here."

"I know." He laughed before shouting, "Can we get some lights in here, please?" I was looking crazy because I didn't see anybody he could possibly be talking to.

All of a sudden the lights came on and people shouted, "Surprise!"

"Corey, what's going on?" I asked while scanning faces to see if I knew anyone. Someone walked up and gave him the mic.

"Drop the banner, please."

On cue the banner dropped, and in bold neon lights I read the words "Chyna's Dolls." I swear my heart dropped when I saw that.

Corey turned to face me. "This is your strip club. I knew you would never pursue your business without your sister, but I couldn't let that happen. I paid for the building and set everything up for you. This is my gift to you. This will allow your sister's memory to live on forever."

All I could do was cry.

"Come on, baby, don't cry. This is a happy moment. Your new beginning."

"Why would you do this for me?"

"Why not? You don't like it?"

I shook my head. "I don't deserve this."

"You deserve this and so much more. Just wait until we walk down that aisle and I bless you with my last name." He grabbed my hand. "Come on, and let's go see your family."

"They're here?" I asked.

"Of course. How could I have your pre-grand opening party without your loved ones?"

He walked me over to where my mom and dad were, and I was so happy to see them. I gave them both a hug and a kiss.

My dad held on to me a little bit longer. "Baby girl, you are very lucky to have Corey. He really loves you, and you know I don't think nobody is good enough for my baby girl. He's a good man for you, so keep him happy." He let me go and looked into my eyes. "I need you to do one thing for me."

"What's that, Papa?"

"You have to let Chyna go, baby. She's gone, and she's not coming back. I know it's hard, believe me, I do. Nothing hurts more than to bury a child. She would want you to be happy, so snap out of that depression and be the strong woman I know you are."

"I'm trying, Daddy. I really am. It's just so hard. She was everything to me."

"Watching your mother give birth to the two of you were my greatest accomplishments, and I vowed I would be in your lives for the rest of my life, no matter how old you got. I always wanted you girls to bury us, not the other way around, but God had other plans." He held my hand. "Get your life together, Blacque Barbee. I can't lose you, too. You need God in your life. I couldn't save Chyna, but I'll be damned if I don't save you." He kissed me on the forehead.

Listening to my father talk damn near broke me down, and I was trying so hard to keep my composure. I had to commend him for his strength, because I know he loved the hell out of Chyna the same way he loved me. At that moment I knew I needed to be strong if I wanted to go on with my life, and I knew I needed to get my life in order.

I felt a tap on my shoulder, and when I turned around it was Mercedes. "Oh, Barbee, I missed you so much. Corey told me you haven't been doing well. I've been trying to see you for weeks now. What's up?"

"I'm sorry, Mercedes. I've been going through it."

"Me too, shit. Chyna was my sister, too."

"I know, and I'm sorry for abandoning you. Where have you been staying?"

"I moved back home with Mom and Pops until they close on the house. We should have the money from it in a few weeks."

"I've been out of touch for real, because I didn't know you moved back home." We walked over and found a seat at an empty table.

"Yeah, after the shooting Papa called me and told me to come home." She shrugged her shoulders. "So, you know, I moved back. He was scared something was going to happen to me, too."

"Yeah, he just gave me a speech about getting my life together and giving it to God." I knew he was right, though. There were so many skeletons in my closet, I knew I needed saving.

Mercedes laughed. "Yeah, he gave me the same speech. He means well, and he does have a point, too."

"I know, right?"

"Girl, so how do you like the club? I know you were surprised." She placed her elbows on the table and waited for my reply.

"Yes, I was. Of course I cried when I saw the name. I don't know how he came up with that name."

Mercedes rocked in her seat. "Well, I'm the one that picked out the name."

Needless to say, I was surprised. "I love it, I really do."

"I just felt it was fitting, and it was a way to keep her a part of our everyday lives. Especially since she was a part of the plan."

"Thanks for being here, Mercedes. You don't know how much this means to me."

"You don't have to say that, girl. That's what sisters are for. Your parents took care of me for years, and that makes us blood, and I love y'all. I knew you needed time to yourself."

I leaned across the table and gave her a hug. "I love you."

"I love you. Now, let's go enjoy this party for Chyna."

We got up and did just that. I had my very first drink in months, and it felt good to loosen up. I danced all night long with Mercedes and Sierra. Corey allowed her to have one drink, and she was mad lit. I was surprised.

Amon and Corey were sitting on the stage, watching us cut up bad. There were two stripper poles on stage, so the three of us made our way up there.

"Sierra, you know how to ride this pole?" I wanted to know if she knew what she was doing.

"Girl, yes, I know what to do. I can teach you a thing or two," she gloated.

"Tuh. I guess you heard that." Mercedes was enjoying this.

"Well, I'm waiting to see what you can do." I placed my hands on my hips. "Let's go, boo."

Sierra handed me her drink and walked up to the pole. She placed her hands around it and walked around it full circle before climbing it and touching the ceiling. Sliding down slowly, she moved her legs like she was pedaling on a bike. I was impressed she was able to do that, and that made me wonder where she learned it from, but that was a conversation for another day. Tonight was about us having a good time.

When it was my turn, I climbed the pole and came down in a split.

Sierra was shouting and jumping up and down. "Girl, where did you learn that from? Let me find out that's why my brother is in love with you."

"You'd be surprised at why your brother loves me."

Sierra looked at Mercedes. "It's your turn."

"Oh no, I'm not getting up there. I'm leaving that to the double-mint twins."

We shared a few more laughs before Corey walked over and interrupted us. "Y'all, come on. I need to make a quick announcement before everyone starts leaving."

He grabbed my hand, and I followed behind him. Mercedes and Sierra sat on the stage.

Corey grabbed the microphone. "Hey, can I have y'all attention for a second?" The DJ cut the music and everybody was silent. "As y'all know, this was a pre-grand opening party for Barbee's strip club, but I cannot leave out a special sister who is part-owner, as well Mercedes. As we all know, these last few months have been very hard with the loss of Chyna, but her memory will live on forever in our hearts and here at Chyna's Dolls." He moved the mic from his mouth and took a deep breath.

"Come on and get it out, bruh," Amon shouted from the crowd.

Corey smiled, then put the mic back to his mouth. "I just want everyone to know how much I love the woman standing next to me."

"I know that's right, brother! Let us know," Sierra shouted, causing me to giggle. She was feeling herself.

"Without further ado." He got down on one knee. "Barbee, I love you, and I cannot imagine living a day on this earth without you as my wife. Will you marry me, please?"

With tears in my eyes, I nodded my head. "Yes."

He placed the ring on my finger and stood up to give me a kiss. We lip-locked for what seemed like five minutes.

"Oh, get a room," Sierra shouted.

"Girl, yo' ass drunk," Mercedes said.

"Girl, I'm so litty," she giggled.

We both heard Sierra, and that broke our kiss because it made us laugh.

"I love your sister, bae. She is crazy, for real."

"Who you telling?" he added.

For the next two hours we threw back a few more drinks and danced until we couldn't dance anymore. Corey had to literally carry Sierra to the car because she was tore down. We followed my parents to their house to make sure they got in safely, and we headed home ourselves.

With all the tragedy that struck all at once, I must say that day was my happy ending. My opening party was a blast thanks to my man and the only sister I have left, along with my family and friends. It was very refreshing to feel so much love under one roof. It had been a while since I felt that. I was also grateful to have a real man in my corner and in my life, because I don't know what I would've done without him.

That night I celebrated many first-time occasions: I was officially the owner of my very first strip club, my first drink in two months, and the best one of them all, Corey got down on one knee in front of my friends and family and asked me to marry him again, but this time with a ring. And of course I said yes, as if it was the very first time.

Chapter 2

Barbee

The next day, when I got up, Corey was gone. He left a note on the nightstand saying he was out handling business and would return soon. Pulling myself from the bed, I got up to look for Sierra since it was mad quiet. I went into her room, but she wasn't there. As soon as I walked past her bathroom, I could hear her coughing violently, so I opened the door. Sierra was on her knees with her head in the toilet, wearing just her bra and panties.

"Yo' ass got a hangover, huh?" I joked before walking over to hold her hair. "Are you okay?"

"No."

"Get up and let me help you to your room." I reached for her, but she pulled away.

"I'm okay. I'll be out in a minute."

I wasn't taking no for an answer, so I pulled her from the floor. "Come on, here."

"Barbee, no, please. Just leave me in here," she snapped.

That wasn't like her. "What's wrong?" I asked.

"Nothing."

She tried to turn her body away from me, and that was when I saw what she was hiding. I leaned down to get a better look to make sure my eyes weren't playing a trick on me. "Sierra, are you pregnant?" She didn't say anything. "Get up!" I screamed.

Sierra rose to her feet and turned to face me. "I'm sorry."

I looked down and it was clear as day: a lifeline going up to her navel on her small baby bump. Seeing her like that took my breath away. All this time she was pregnant and I never noticed it, and of course she failed to mention it. I guessed that was because I had been wallowing in my own sorrow. Looking at her broke my heart.

"Is it Dre's baby?"

She nodded her head up and down. "Yes."

"Wow!" I sighed.

"I'm sorry, Barbee. I didn't want you to find out like this. I know what you're going through, so I was just waiting on the right time."

"So, Corey knows about this?"

"No, I haven't told him. I didn't have the nerve to tell him, either. With everything that's been going on, I didn't want to add to the stress," she pleaded.

"Does Dre know?" I was trying to figure out what had been going on during my mental absence.

"Nobody knows."

This was too much to take in, so I walked out without saying another word. Back in my bedroom, I closed the door and sat on the bed, thinking about how we were going to get through this little dilemma. The way my mind was setup, there was no way she was keeping that baby. I didn't care if I had to take her to the abortion clinic myself. That baby was leaving this world, and I knew Corey would agree.

After sitting in the same spot for the next ten minutes, there was a knock on the door. I knew it was Sierra, so I didn't say anything. She stood there for a good sixty seconds before she walked in.

"Barbee, can I come in, please?"

I ignored her, but that didn't stop her from coming in and sitting down beside me. "I know you probably hate me right now, but I never meant for this to happen. What am I gon' do with a baby? I don't know the first thing about being a mother."

A lone tear fell from my eye and down my cheek. I knew she didn't do it on purpose, but it still hurt like hell.

"Barbee, don't shut me out, please." She paused. "I need you."

My silence made her give up on trying to get through to me. Sierra stood up and looked down at me. "If this pregnancy is going to lead to you not talking to me, then I will have an abortion. I love you, Barbee, and I don't want to see you hurting because of me. I'll make the appointment now." She said her final words and walked away.

It hurt me to hurt her, so I spoke up. "Sierra, wait."

She stopped in her tracks, but she didn't turn around.

"Come back." I stood up, and when she was close, I hugged her. "I'm sorry."

She hugged me tight. "You don't have to apologize."

"Yes, I do. It's not your fault I'm going through this. My very own actions put me in this situation, and I shouldn't make you feel bad about it." We held each other and cried.

"So, you forgive me?"

"Of course. You didn't do anything wrong." I released her from my arms and looked at her. "Well, you didn't use a condom. That's about it." I laughed to lighten up the mood.

"Tell me about it," she responded. "Now I have to tell Corey, and he's going to lose it."

"Don't you worry about Corey. I'll handle him. In the meantime, you just make sure our baby is healthy. So, no more drinking for you."

Sierra laughed. "Don't worry. I won't drink any more liquor." She paused. "You're saying I should keep the baby?"

"Yes. I can't make you have an abortion. Babies are blessings."

"What about Dre and his wife?"

"Let us worry about that. You just focus on you and Peanut in there." I rubbed her stomach.

"Peanut?" Sierra's eyebrows furrowed with astonishment. "Ew."

"Yeah, that's cute."

"No, it's not," she laughed. "Thanks for being the best sister a girl could ask for." She hugged me once more.

"What did I just walk in on?" Corey asked, causing both of us to jump.

"I didn't hear you come in," I replied.

"I'm a smooth criminal, baby." He walked over to us. "So, what's going on?" he asked again.

I knew Corey like a book, and I knew he wasn't going to let this go without an answer. What I also knew was not to keep any secrets from him, so he might as well get the truth. There was no need in keeping this away from him. Sierra was afraid, I could tell by her demeanor and the way she played with her fingers. It was now or never.

"Sierra has something to tell you." She looked up at me and shook her no. "Go ahead. We're gonna get through this together." I grabbed her hand. "I promise."

"Get through what?" Corey asked.

Sierra stood behind me. "I'm pregnant," she whispered.

Corey took a step closer. "You're what?"

"Pregnant." We both studied his face, but were unable to determine what he was thinking.

The next thing I knew, he reached across me and snatched Sierra by her shirt. "You pregnant from that no-good-ass nigga, Dre?" He pulled her closer to him. "How could you be so stupid?" he spat.

I had to intervene. I couldn't let him do her like that. "Corey, stop." Squeezing my way in the middle, I grabbed his hand and pried her shirt from his grip. "Baby, please, calm down."

"Fuck that. What the hell she gon' do with a baby? She hasn't even graduated yet."

I knew he was upset, but this was not helping the situation at all. "I know you're upset, but we need to be here for her."

"Fuck that." Corey released her and stepped back. "This nigga gotta see me. I'ma kill his ass."

Now he wasn't thinking at all. "And what is that gonna solve? You want her to be a single mother?"

"Nah, she getting rid of that baby."

"And what if she doesn't want to?" I added.

"She doesn't have a choice."

Sierra finally spoke up. "I want to keep it."

She caught him off guard. "For what? That ain't gon' make the nigga want you. Babies don't keep a nigga."

I stood there shaking my head as Sierra broke down and cried. "That's not why I want this baby. I don't give a fuck about him after what he did to me."

"Then what the fuck you want a baby for?" Corey barked, sending a chill down my spine.

Sierra took a deep breath. "For you and Barbee. I told her I would have an abortion, but she said I didn't have to."

He then looked at me. "What the fuck you told her that for?"

I simply stated, "I don't believe in abortions."

"Well, I do in fucked-up circumstances."

"Can you stop being selfish for a second?" I could tell this argument was about to get nasty. "Think about someone else's feelings for a second."

"That's easy for you to say, because I have to be the one taking care of the bastard."

He had officially drawn the line. Sierra wasn't able to defend herself, but I could. I had to step in closer so he could feel where I was coming from. "Let me tell you something. I'm not gon' sit back and listen to you talk to her like that. She's been through enough already."

He was about to respond, but Sierra cut him off. "The only reason I was keeping the baby was because of what happened to y'all baby. What if Barbee can never have another baby?" She looked over at me. "What if this is the only chance y'all have? At least the baby would have good parents." She dropped her gaze to floor, staring at her wiggling toes. "I'm sorry I messed up everything. I guess you gon' send me back to the group home."

"We're not sending you anywhere." I replied.

Sierra left us both there, standing in our thoughts, and went to her room.

This was the first time I was disgusted by Corey's actions. If looks could kill, he would have been laid out on the floor. "Are you happy now? You just made this situation worse than it already is."

He walked over to the bed and sat down, burying his head in his hands. "I fucked up, didn't I?"

I walked over to him and placed my hand on his shoulder. "It's not too late to fix it." Kneeling down, we made eye contact. "I know you're upset, but you have to put yourself in her shoes. She's sixteen and pregnant from a married man. You know she already feels bad. We just have to deal with this the best way we can."

"Bae, I don't know how."

"That's what I'm here for. I promise we'll make this work."

"I wanted her to go to college and make a better life for herself," he admitted.

"And she can still do that with our help. Having a baby is not the end of the world."

"I don't know, baby."

"We got this, and Dre punk-ass gon' help with this baby."

"You damn right he is."

"Now, go talk to her and apologize for your outburst."

Corey looked at me with those tantalizing eyes, and it made me forget I was mad at him. "Can you come with me? I need moral support."

"Really, babe?"

"I'm new to this emotional thing."

I grabbed his hand and smiled. "Come on, let's go."

When we walked into Sierra's room, she was packing her bags. "What are you doing?" Corey asked. This was his moment to make things right, so I kept quiet.

"Getting out of your hair so you don't have to take care of me and my bastard," she snapped.

I nudged him in the back and he walked over to stop her from packing. "I'm sorry, Sierra. I overreacted. I should've never said those things to you. It caught me off guard."

"Yeah, I see."

"I don't want you to leave."

"That's not how I feel." She looked at him and tears fell from her eyes. "You said some hurtful things to me."

"I know, and that's why I'm apologizing." He grabbed her hand and sat down on her bed. "From the time you were born I knew I had to protect you, and that's what I'm trying to do. I missed out on your life, and all I want to do is make up for lost time. I just want the best for you, and I know having this baby is going to mess that up."

"It won't, Corey, I promise. I want to go to college, and I won't let this deter me from what I need to do. I'll even get a job."

"No, you won't. Your job is to get good grades. Me, Barbee, and punk-ass Dre will take care of this baby so you can focus."

"I doubt if Dre does anything." She hadn't spoken to him since the wedding brawl, either.

Corey chuckled. "Oh, that nigga gon' do his job, and you can bet that." He played with the hair on his chin. "As a matter of fact, I'm gon' call the nigga, and we all gon' have a sit-down."

Sierra smiled. "Okay."

Corey stood up and hugged his sister. "I love you, and everything is going to be okay. Big bruh got you, okay?"

"I love you, too. And thank you." Sierra winked at me.

Corey and I went into our bedroom. Slamming the door behind us, he walked past me in a hurry. "I'm 'bouta call this bitch-ass nigga," he said.

"Bae, don't you think you should wait until tomorrow, after you have calmed down?" I knew he could be irrational, and I didn't want him to make things worse by strong-arming him. That could push Dre away.

"Fuck that, he need to hear me now." Corey grabbed his phone off the dresser and hit him up, placing it on speaker.

I remained silent and sat down on the edge of the bed because I didn't want to start an argument with my man over that nigga.

"Yeah," Dre answered.

"Nigga, you got my muthafuckin' sister pregnant." His jaw was clenched tight, and the scowl on his face would scare a dyke bitch straight.

"What?" Dre seemed confused.

"You heard what the fuck I said." Corey's bark was just as big as his bite.

"You gon' tell me what you said or not? I ain't on that fuck-shit today," Dre barked back with the same amount of aggression.

"My sister pregnant, nigga."

There was a long pause. "Damn, man. She told you that?" Dre's voice softened a bit.

"What the fuck you think."

"I'm asking you, shit. What, you want me to pay for the abortion?" Dre asked.

"Nah, you gon' step the fuck up and be a father to your child."

"Fuck!" Dre's voice boomed through the receiver. "How I'm supposed to explain this shit to Tokee?"

"I don't give a fuck how you tell her, just make sure she knows. And if you won't tell her, I will. You should've thought about that shit when you was fuckin' my sister."

"Nigga, you act like I knew that. All these years we ran together I never knew you had one, so stop acting like I went behind your back on some creep shit and got at yo' sister."

"Just do what the fuck I said." Corey hung up the phone and tossed it on the bed.

His nose flared out like a raging bull. I walked over and grabbed him around the waist. His muscles were tense and his breathing was heavy, as his chest rose up and down. I needed to get him calm, so I did what a real bitch would do when her nigga was having a bad day.

"Relax, baby, I got you."

I dropped down to my knees and slowly pulled down his pants and boxers until they were at his feet. Making my way back north, I used my finger to draw an invisible trail from his leg up to his inner thigh. The moment my hands gripped his soft dick, stroking it twice, he rocked up immediately. I took every inch of his thick dick into my mouth and locked my jaw.

***

A few days passed, and Corey delivered on his promise. We were seated outside at a patio table at the Cheesecake Factory awaiting Tokee and Dre's arrival.

Corey played with his silverware. "I know this fuck-nigga ain't standing me up, 'cause if so, I'm dumping two slugs in his chest, and that's on God."

"He's gon' show up, babe. Relax," I said while stroking his back.

"For his sake, he better."

Before I could say anything else, I looked toward the door and in walked Dre with Tokee on his heels.

"Sorry we late," Dre apologized as he gave Corey a handshake. Afterward he looked at Sierra and held her stare.

Tokee folded her arms across her chest. "Are you gon' pull my chair out, or what?"

Dre pulled her chair out, then sat down beside her. His focus went back to Sierra. "How you doing?"

"Fine." I knew Sierra wasn't feeling the fact Tokee had to be there, but I let her know it was necessary if Dre was going to be part of the child's life. There had to be a common ground since they were married and he would eventually have the child sleep over. But see, I knew Tokee, and I knew she wasn't like that, but in situations like this a person never knew what someone was capable of. There was going to be plenty of time to get things sorted out by the time the baby was old enough to stay overnight.

Awkward silence floated in the air.

"We haven't ordered yet. We were waiting on y'all."

"Thanks, B." Dre picked up his menu and looked it over for a few minutes.

The waitress came back to the table shortly after their arrival and took our drink and food orders. As soon as she walked away, Corey couldn't wait to get to the point.

"We all know why we here, so let's just cut to the chase. The last time we were around each other it wasn't pleasant, but times and situations have changed." Corey cleared his throat and smirked at Dre. "I don't like the fact my sister is pregnant from you, but I know you will take care of your responsibilities as a man, 'cause if you don't, me and you gon' have problems."

Dre sat up in his seat. He wasn't feeling the way Corey was trying to punk him in front of his wife and Sierra. "Bruh, you ain't gotta do all that. I'm here, ain't I? I already told you I'm gon' be there for my shorty."

Tokee snapped her head back and looked at Dre. "What the fuck did you just say?"

Dre avoided eye contact with her. "She's pregnant with my baby."

"And you thought it was okay to bring me here for this bullshit? How could you do this to me? Fucking her wasn't enough? You had to get her pregnant, too?" Tokee's eyes became glassy, and my heart broke for her.

Corey shook his head. "I told you to tell her before I did."

"Dre, you could've told me this shit at home instead of embarrassing me more than you already have." Tokee's voice cracked as she tried to hold back her tears.

Dre looked at her. "I'm sorry. I just didn't know how to tell you. I've hurt you so many times."

"Obviously not enough," Tokee cried, picking up the napkin from the table and dabbing her eyes.

When I looked to the other side of the patio, I noticed a woman staring. "We have to keep it down before they kick us out. This is a delicate situation, and we all need to be adults

Destiny Skai

without the unnecessary drama. Whether we like it or not, a baby will be here within the next six or seven months."

"You need to apologize to my sister." Corey had no sympathy for what Dre was going through. His only concern was Sierra, and I knew that. Hell, we all did.

Dre didn't argue with him, instead he turned to face Sierra. "I'm sorry for everything I put you through. I know I lied to you in the past, but I'm gon' be here for you and the baby." Tokee coughed in an effort to interrupt his little speech, so he looked back at her. "Man, stop all that bullshit. The truth is out, and it ain't shit I can do about it. All we can do is move forward. The last thing I need is more stress."

I guess he told her, 'cause after that she sat back in her seat and looked in the opposite direction. I couldn't really blame her 'cause I knew I would be pissed, too, but she knew he cheated with her, and yet she stayed even after her wedding was ruined. At the end of the day, she was gon' have to accept the fact he had a baby on her or move on with her life.

I sipped my drink and watched this Lifetime series play out in front of me. Every so often I would glance at Corey, then at Tokee to see her facial expression. Eventually she got tired of listening to him and stood up. "You know what, Dre? You are absolutely right. You don't need any more stress in your life. So, I tell you what, I'm going to help you become stress free. I'm leaving."

Dre looked up at her. "Come on, Tokee, stop it. You know exactly what I mean."

"Nah, I really don't." Tokee chuckled, but it wasn't funny. It was more of a sinister laugh. "You think I'ma sit here and watch you apologize to the female that ruined our marriage? You must be fuckin' crazy. You don't even know if that's your baby or not."

As soon as those words left her lips, Sierra sat her drink down on the table and looked Tokee up and down. "First off, bitch, you don't know shit about me, but your husband do. He knows me very well, inside and out. Dre broke my virginity, and we never used a condom, so he know what it is. You just mad because your child was a slip-up and he wasn't ready to be a daddy." Sierra sat back and laughed. I knew Dre had been pillow-talking with her about Tokee, because what she stated was a fact. When Tokee found out she was pregnant, Dre wanted her to have an abortion because the timing was wrong.

Tokee's brow rose just a little. She cocked back and slapped Dre dead in the mouth. "You told her our business? That's how you get down now? Fuck you, Dre, and your bastard-ass child. Don't come home, 'cause you no longer have one with me." Tokee picked up her drink off the table and threw the contents in Dre's face. Surprisingly, he didn't say a word or react to her rant. He simply picked up the cloth napkin from the table and wiped his face.

Seeing her like that made me feel bad, so I got up and gave chase.

Tokee found a secluded area on the outside of the restaurant and sat down. I took a seat next to her. "I'm sorry you have to go through this, but it's the right thing to do."

I could see the tears building up in her eyes. "You don't care."

"I wouldn't be sitting here if I didn't," I answered truthfully.

"I heard about what happened to you and Chyna, and I'm sorry for your loss. I came to see you in the hospital, but you were out of it. And I also attended the funeral, but not the burial."

Hearing that took me back to that awful day, but I had to keep my composure. "Oh. I didn't know that," I answered, holding back my tears.

She continued, "I left after the final viewing because I didn't know how you would react to me being there."

"I wouldn't have said anything, but thanks for coming."

"So, how have you been? I've been worried about you." Her words were sincere, and I could feel it in my soul.

"Just taking it one day at a time. Some days are harder than others, but I'm dealing with it."

"I know that feeling all too well. I don't know what to do, Barbee." She dropped her head as if her thoughts were weighing her down. "I'm so lost, and the only person I had to talk to was you. Now I have nobody, and I just keep everything bottled in. I don't even talk to my sister anymore. Not since the wedding."

In my mind I knew they were gon' resort to that. Her sister loved every chance she got to talk bad about their relationship. I'm the type of person to give advice, and what she does from there is on her. I never tried to convince her to leave Dre. If she wanted to stay, that was on her, 'cause there was a time when no one could tell me anything about Meat. I truly felt her pain.

"Tokee, I know what you're going through 'cause I've been there before. You have to do what's best for you and your child. If you want to be with Dre, you have to forgive him for what he's done and move on. I know it hurts, but that's what you have to do if you stay."

She looked at me with her tear-streaked makeup on her face. "I love him to death, B."

"I know you do. This is not an overnight decision, so give it some deep thought. Just remember: if you stay, you can't throw it up in his face whenever you're mad. You have to let it go and accept that child and treat it like it's your own."

"That's my biggest problem. I can forgive the cheating, but he has an outside child now. Do you know how that's gon' make me look?"

Before I knew it, my tongue slipped, but I didn't lie. "It won't be no worse than what happened at the wedding. This is one of the consequences of cheating. Just be glad it wasn't some shit you couldn't get rid of, like AIDS."

"I know, but—"

I cut her off. "There's no but, and stop worrying about what people think. Opinions are like assholes; everybody has one. None of them are paying your bills, so fuck what they think."

Tokee finally smiled. "See, that's what I miss, our long talks and that I-don't-give-a-fuck attitude you possess. I wish I had that."

"You have it. You just need to let it out," I laughed. It was gonna be a cold day in hell before we saw that day.

"I'm sorry, Barbee. I miss you, and I should've reached out to you sooner. You are my closest friend, and I want our relationship back."

"I miss you, too, and you don't have to apologize," I honestly stated. Not only did I miss her doing my hair, but I missed her as a friend. She had always been loyal to me.

"I do, because I thought you knew about their relationship after all this time. It was Dre who told me you didn't know and I was mad at you for nothing."

"It's all good, because I know how it looked. I should've reached out to you, as well, and explained everything to you."

Tokee leaned over and gave me a hug. I embraced her back. I had a feeling everything from there would be okay and we all would become one big, happy family.

Destiny Skai

Chapter 3

Barbee

After dealing with Sierra and Dre's dilemma, I decided to take a break from the family drama and get some me-time. I rode smoothly through traffic listening to Rick Ross's *Apple of My Eye*. Everything on that album was truth, but this was my favorite song. It was just me and my car, ready to blast at anything that tried it.

Since I got shot, my radar was on high beam. I was always aware of my surroundings, but that day I slipped, and it cost me my child and my sister's life. Never again would I let that happen to me or the ones I loved. In my eyes everyone was a suspect. I didn't trust a soul walking outside of my peeps, and that's G-shit.

Interrupting my gangster thoughts was my cellphone. I sucked my teeth when I saw who was calling, but I picked up anyway. I knew if I didn't, he would blow me up back-to-back.

"Hello." I was trying to cover the disgust in my voice.

"You don't fuck with me no more, I see?" Rich asked.

It was funny how I was so into him, and now I couldn't stand his ass. I no longer had use for him, so there was no need in pretending. "I answered, didn't I?"

"Yeah, but you have an attitude."

"Because I'm not with the bullshit today. I don't have the time or the energy to argue with you."

"I'm not trying to argue. I'm just trying to see what's up with my girl since she up and disappeared on a nigga."

"Rich, I'm not your girl, and you know that. What we had is over."

"What the fuck you mean, *what we had is over?*" he yelled into the phone.

"You need to lower your voice when you talking to me. I don't know what the fuck your problem is." I didn't know who this nigga thought he was talking to, but he had the wrong bitch. He was two seconds from talking to the dial tone.

"You my problem. All you wanna do is lead a nigga on, and I ain't on that fuck-shit."

"I didn't lead you on then, and I'm not leading you on now. You haven't seen me in over two months, so how do you figure that?"

"You think you just gon' come into my life and give me some of that good pussy and walk away? You got me fucked up."

I wanted to laugh so bad 'cause the man was clearly on some bug shit. If I didn't know any better, I would think this nigga was pussy-whipped, and I wasn't even fucking him like that. Now I could see why he was single. This muthafucka was crazy as a betsy bug. "Listen, Rich, it's over between us, and I don't want to be with you. So, I advise you walk away peacefully, because I'm not what you think I am. You really don't wanna be fucked up with a female like me."

This nigga had the nerve to bust out laughing. "You sound so sexy when you mad."

"I'm not mad. I just want you to respect my mind and my space."

"And you need to respect the fact I'm telling you it's not over until I say it's over. I made big plans for our future."

"Well, I'm sorry you did that, but we don't have a future together. I don't want to be with you." This man was not taking no for an answer.

"You're in denial."

"No, you're delusional if you think we have a future after not seeing or hearing from me after two months. If we were together, that would've never happened."

"Sounds like you found a new man."

"Bye, Rich. I'm not doing this with you. Have a nice life."

"Bitch, I'll kill you if you hang up on me."

That was the last straw, so I hung up the phone. This nigga had the nerve to call me out and threaten me. Seconds later he was calling me back-to-back, so I put him on call block. After a few times of getting the voicemail, he sent me a text message.

You fucked with the wrong one, and you'll see me soon. I love you, Barbee. How could you do this to me? All I wanted to do was give you everything your heart desires and you would shit on me like that? You are a heartless and cruel bitch!! I hate you.

After reading the message, I deleted it because I wasn't about to give him the reaction he was looking for. Clearly he couldn't take rejection. My phone beeped once more. It was another text message.

I'm sorry, bae, I didn't mean any of that. I love you!

I deleted that message, too. "What the fuck wrong with this nigga?" I mumbled. He was really on one. Never in a million years did I think Rich would be this type of dude — the type that was possessive and would beat your ass on a daily basis for any little thing. Something told me I dodged one hell of a bullet. I was grateful I never brought him to where I lived or to my neck of the woods. The only thing he knew was I was from Lauderdale. However, I would need to keep an extra set of eyes open for him because I didn't take threats lightly, and something told me he had stalker tendencies.

My activities for the day consisted of a little pampering. I was well overdue for my eyebrows, lashes, nails and pedicure. All of that took two hours, and I was well on my way into the world. When I walked out of the shop, I felt refreshed and like new money. That was one thing that made every woman in America happy: getting pampered.

***

It had been a while since I visited my parents' house, and it was time that I did that.

"Look what the cat dragged in," Mercedes laughed as I walked into her bedroom at my parents' house.

"Is that how you greet me after not seeing me for a few days?" I closed the door and sat down on the bed next to her.

"Yes, 'cause you don't do me no more. You over there playing step-mama and shit." Mercedes turned the volume down on the television.

I couldn't help but laugh. "Girl, that would have to be his daughter in order for her to be my step-child." I shook my head. "You retarded."

"Well, you know what I mean. Shit, yo' ass be missing, and I'm surprised to see you. I'm happy, but surprised."

"Yeah, I bet. So, what's going on?" I asked.

"You know me, I slide from here to there." She sat upright in the bed with her back against the headboard. "I got me a li'l snack."

"You still calling dudes snacks?"

"Would you like it better if I called him *zaddy*?"

"Well, that's the new trend now, I see."

"You know I don't follow trends. I set them," she laughed.

"I know that's right. Well, I got a call from the realtor, and she will be showing the house today at 4:00 p.m. If she can't get a buyer within the next two weeks, they're going to hold an open house."

"Good, 'cause I want my money." Mercedes rubbed her hands together.

"Shit, me too." Scratching my head, I looked at her closely. "Are you moving with the money?"

"Yeah, I'm buying a condo with it. I don't need a house since it's just me."

She looked over at the bookshelf that housed a picture of the four of us during our happy days, and a single teardrop rolled down her cheek. Our wounds were still fresh, and so was the pain. My chest rose and fell as my body prepared for the breakdown I was about to endure. Tears filled my eyes, and there was the domino effect. We held each other tight.

"I miss her so much, Mercedes."

"I do, too. We were supposed to move to Palm Beach and start over together. Now I'm going to be all alone." She sobbed loudly. "What am I supposed to do without her?"

"We have to move on and keep her memory alive. It's going to be hard, but we'll get through this together." I was finally taking the advice my pops gave me. All I had to do now was make it happen. This was going to be a hard process, but there was nothing we could do to bring her back, 'cause trust and believe I would give up every dollar to see my sister again.

After rocking and crying, we finally let go of one another. I had to admit that was the best cry ever, and to be honest I felt a weight lift off my shoulders. My father was right: I needed to let her go and move on with my life. That didn't mean forget about her. It just meant I had to learn to live without her. There was just one last thing I had to do before I moved on completely, and that was kill the muthafucka responsible for my family's pain and suffering.

***

Rich

This bitch had no idea who she was fucking with. She had a nigga like me fucked up, especially if she thought I was gon' let her walk away so easily. I paced my living room in a circle, trying to figure out how to find her. This girl never took me to her house, but I knew where she was from, and I had her license plate number. That wasn't gon' do me any good if I couldn't get someone to look it up for me, but I didn't give a damn. If I had to ride the streets of Lauderdale day and night until I found her, then that's what I was prepared to do.

I took my phone out, scrolled through the gallery, and located some pics I snuck of her when she was sleeping or not paying attention. Suddenly, my mom's number flashed across my screen, interrupting my trip down memory lane.

"Yeah." I was not in the mood to talk to her. I was no longer a child, and she couldn't tell me what to do. I knew that's exactly what she was calling for.

"You don't sound happy to hear from your mother," she said.

"I'm actually busy right now," I replied.

"Oh, what are you doing?"

"I'm minding my business, that's what I'm doing." I walked into the kitchen because I was desperately trying to keep from cursing her out. Opening up the drawer, I pulled out my stress ball and squeezed it.

"Is that how you talk to me now?" The sarcasm was thick in her voice, and I was on the verge of blowing a head gasket.

"I always talk to you like this, so don't act like this is new." That damn ball was not working for me. "Anyway, how can I help you, Brenda?"

She laughed in the phone. "I'm Brenda now? Am I making you mad?"

I closed my eyes tightly. "Listen, stop fucking with me and tell me what you want."

Brenda sighed. "Well, I was calling because you haven't been to see your doctor, because they just called me and, judging by your tone, I can tell you are off your meds."

"Fuck you and that doctor. Both of y'all can suck my dick."

I bammed it on that ho 'cause she had me fucked up. I'm a grown-ass man, and nobody-ass man, and nobody was about to tell me how to live my life. I took my meds when I got ready, and not when a bitch told me too. Brenda completely ruined my mood, and I needed a woman to talk to. Well, not just any woman – Barbee.

What was so strange about it all was Barbee resembled my mother when she was younger, and that made it much easier to fall in love with her and hate her in some instances. It brought me back to the days of when I really loved my mother as a young boy and how much I despised her as a teen.

When I looked at my messages to her, I just stood there feeling a headache coming on. I placed the stress ball back in the drawer and grabbed me a Gatorade from the fridge. My mood was fucked up all over again because I knew she had placed me on the blocked list, especially after the way I talked to her. Maybe I should take my meds after all.

I left the kitchen and went into my hall closet to retrieve my meds. Pulling the bag down, I looked through it and pulled out the Risperdal. My mother was the only one who knew about my condition, and that was the way I planned on keeping it.

When I was 17 years old, I was diagnosed with borderline personality disorder. All I remember is reaching the highlight of my life and, in the blink of an eye, it was all over.

I was the captain of the football team. Every girl in the school wanted me and would drop their drawers with no hesitation. My teammates were jealous that my pussy rate was higher than theirs, but it wasn't a big deal. Or so I thought.

One day after school they invited me to chill. I was down for it, so I went with them. We went by this dude named Bobby's house since his mom was at work. When we got there, there was plenty of booze and beer. We had a few shots of Jack Daniels and played a few games of beer pong. We were fucked up. Bobby and two others indulged in some Acid, but I turned that down. Then, out the blue, Bobby pulls out a pre-rolled joint for us to smoke.

At first I was reluctant to hit it, but peer pressure was a muthafucka. After a few hits, I felt lightheaded. I didn't know if I was coming or going. All the boys except one began to laugh at my behavior, but I was clueless.

I tried to pass it, but nobody wanted it.

The suspense and their secret alliance had me feeling uncomfortable, so I left on foot to find the nearest bus stop. Everything around me was moving fast, and I often found myself running from nobody in particular. The sun was extremely hot, and my shirt was drenched in sweat, as I made it to some shade. I pulled my shirt over my head and tried to catch my breath. As soon as I made it home, I went to my room, and that's all I could remember.

A few hours later, my mother came into my room, shaking me from a weird dream, and I can remember the conversation as if it happened yesterday. She sat on the edge of my bed.

"You know I love you, right?"

I was anxious to see where the lecture was going. Every time I did something wrong, that was how she started her sentence. "Yes, Ma, I know that." *Looking in her eyes, I could see she was about to tear up, so I placed my hand on top of hers.* "Ma, what's wrong?"

"I'm sorry I have to do this to you, but it's the only way I can help you," *she cried.*

"Ma, what are you talking about?"

She stood up, and I could see a fresh bruise on her face. "You have to go with these people, Richard. They're gonna help you."

"Who, ma? And what happened to your face?"

She walked away, and when she opened the door, two police officers were standing there.

"What the fuck y'all want?"

"Just come with us, son," *one of them spoke up.*

"I'm not going anywhere with y'all, so get the fuck out of here. Ma, what's going on? Why you let them in here?" *My anger and aggression elevated quickly.*

"You need to calm down and put your shoes on. You can come voluntary or involuntarily," *the officer responded in a vile tone.*

"The only way I'm leaving is if you drag me out this bitch." *My tone matched his.*

Before I knew it, he ran up on me, grabbed me by the shoulders, and threw me onto the bed.

"Stop resisting, Richard. They're only trying to help you."

He pulled my arms behind my back and slapped the cuffs on. "You call this help? This ain't no fuckin' help."

"You shouldn't have put your hands on your mother, and you wouldn't be going with us right now, so shut your mouth." *He was applying so much pressure I could feel my arms go numb.*

45

"I would never put my hands on my mother. Are you stu-pid?" That shit wasn't making any sense because I loved my mother, and I would never hurt her.

"Look at her face and tell me you didn't do that," the officer pulled me up and shouted in my face. I looked at her for confirmation, and all she could do was cry as they hauled me out of the house and into the backseat of the patrol car. For the life of me, I couldn't understand what had gone wrong.

My mother trailed us until we arrived to the Ft. Lauderdale Hospital, which was located downtown by Las Olas, a popular tourist and hangout spot. Once they took me in, I learned I was being Baker Acted and wouldn't be released until 72 hours later, if I was medically stable. That sent me into a rage. I was kicking over the chairs and throwing items because I was upset my mother would allow something so heinous to happen to me. The medical staff attacked me and placed me into a strait jacket, saying I was harmful to myself and those around me.

They placed me in a padded room for a few hours, but I was let out eventually to see the psychiatrist. That's when I was informed about the attack on my mother. Apparently I came home from school and she confronted me about smelling like weed and liquor. I became aggressive toward her, and there was a tussle. She slapped me to bring me to my senses, but that's when I became more violent toward her and punching her in the face. I recall the bruise on her face, but I couldn't recollect my actions that evening.

After 72 hours I returned to school and there was so much chatter going on, but no one would fill me in. I was ignored and brushed off by everyone, including the girls that were on my trail. At the end of the day, I was approached by the silent dude from the group, Mark, and he gave me an earful on what was going on. Apparently Bobby had laced the joint with PCP, which caused me to flip my lid. Bobby also went around the

46

school telling the other students what was going on. What made it worse was the fact he recorded it on his cellphone and was able to show me the footage. I could feel my chest tighten and rage fill my body. The only thing on my mind was fucking Bobby up on sight.

"Send that to my phone," I instructed Mark. That was all the proof I needed to show I was drugged.

"Okay," Mark replied.

"Good looking out, man." I threw my book bag over my shoulder. "I have practice, so I'll get at you later." Mark looked as if he had something heavy on his mind, other than what he told me, so I probed a little more. "What's going on, man?"

"I don't know how to tell you this."

Now he definitely had my attention. "Tell me what?"

"They kicked you off the team."

That was the kicker. Football was my life, and I lost that, too, behind a venomous snake, but I wasn't going down without a fight. Literally.

A few days later I caught up with Bobby and beat the brakes off him, sending him to the ICU unit in the hospital. When the police arrived, I showed them the video footage and my case went under an extensive investigation. Weeks later the charges against me were dropped, and Bobby ended up in a juvenile detention center.

Things were finally looking up until I was evaluated and diagnosed with a personality disorder. To this day I blamed my mother because she should have never sent me to a mental facility. It seemed like it did me more harm than good.

My trip down memory lane came to a halt so I could take my meds. I popped two Risperdal into my mouth and went into my bedroom to lie down. It was raining outside, which caused my body to shut down and relax. A nap was what I needed.

As I slowly faded away into la-la land, the melody from my cellular device stirred me from my sleep. My heart skipped a beat, hoping it was Barbee. Disappointment hit me hard when I realized it wasn't her calling me back. Instead, it was the head honcho, Giovanni.

"Whadup, G?"

"I need you to come by the house. It's important."

"Everything good with the business?"

"We'll talk. Just get here soon."

"A'ight. I'm on the way."

***

As I pulled up to the estate, I knew it was a serious matter because Giovanni was sitting outside on the porch, twirling his Chinese Baoding iron balls in his right hand. The first thing on my mind was robbery, or a bitch-ass nigga ran his mouth to the folks and the heat was on. I parked the car and killed the ignition, hopping out quickly to see what the deal was.

"Shit must be bad for you to be sitting out here."

"You have no idea." He stood up. "Let's go inside." I followed Giovanni to his study.

His little henchmen were posted up with their hands folded in front of them, so I knew shit was crucial. When I sat down, Mattie walked up and stood to the side of me. Gio took his seat and folded his hands on top of his desk.

"Since we've met, I've treated you like a son, correct?"

"Correct." I wasn't really sure where this was going, but something told me this was about me. The last person that sat me down like this was my mother right before she handed me over to the authorities.

"I'm going to ask you a question, and I want the God's honest truth from you." The cold stare in his eyes sent a feeling over me that I've never felt before. It was a look of betrayal. "Or you and I are going to have a problem."

"I've been honest and loyal to you from day one." Now my thoughts were running a marathon in my brain.

"How long did you know Barbee before you brought her to my house?"

The sound of her name made me feel uneasy. I needed to know why he was so concerned about her. "Not that long. Why, what's up?"

"So you brought a complete stranger into my home?"

"That was my girl, so I thought it was cool."

Giovanni sat back in his chair and rocked. "Where is she now?"

"I don't know. We had a fight, so I haven't spoken to her. What's going on?"

"About two and a half months ago, when I went out of town, my product came up missing. Someone broke into my home and stole everything from my closet."

"And you're just telling me?"

"I needed to get proof before I jumped the gun."

"Wait, you think she had something to do with that?"

"I know for a fact she had something to do with it. Now, the next thing I need to know is if you put her up to it?"

The accusations he just put on me were absurd. I had never taken anything from him. "I don't know what you're talking about."

Mattie placed his gun on my temple. "Don't lie to my uncle, or there's gonna be brain splatter everywhere. You got that?"

Although there was a gun to my temple, I ignored what he was talking about because he wasn't pulling no trigger without his uncle's permission. "Come on, man, I know you don't think I would ever cross you like that? Since I've been dealing with you, have I ever come up short or took anything from you?"

He took a minute to think before he answered me. "That's why I brought you here, to talk to you face-to-face like a man and look in your eyes when you answer me."

"And what have you observed?"

"That you might be telling the truth." He nodded his head toward Mattie. "Put the gun down."

I knew that was a lie. "If you didn't believe me, you would've let him kill me by now."

"That may be true, but what I need from you is to find Barbee and bring her to me. That will prove to me you are loyal, like you say you are, and you had nothing to do with it."

I wasn't feeling what he was saying. To bring her to him was like me pulling the trigger on her myself. If he had proof, I needed to know what it was. "Why are you so certain it was her?"

He stopped rocking in his chair and looked deep into my eyes. "Because her friend told me before I had Mattie shoot her in the mouth."

I swear my heart stopped for a moment because I knew exactly who he was talking about. "You killed her?"

"Without a second thought."

I was in disbelief. "Damn."

"I asked her if you knew anything about it, and she said you were a target from the beginning. Looks like she set you up. Do you know where to find her?"

"No."

"Mattie, give him the address."

Now it all made sense why she stopped accepting my calls. That bitch set me up for the kill. The love I had for her turned into pure hate. How could she do me like that? One thing was guaranteed to happen at this point: I was about to pay Barbee's ass a visit, and I wasn't gon' rest until I had her in my possession. She crossed the line, and now she was gon' pay.

Destiny Skai

Chapter 4

Barbee

Selling this house has been a task within itself. As soon as they realize there was a shootout here, they stop the continuation process out of fear the house won't be safe. I walked room-to-room, reminiscing on the good times we had here. Unfortunately, it all came to an end. I guess that's one of the consequences of being greedy, and it was all on me. If I would've never convinced them to rob Giovanni, Chyna would still be here.

I stood at the door of the room that belonged to her and just stared, imagining she was lying in bed. As bad as I wanted to cry, I couldn't pull myself to do it.

The realtor was standing outside speaking to potential buyers. Hopefully this would be the last couple to see the house, and they would be closing out soon. I couldn't stand to come back.

Sudden movement behind me caused me to jump. When I spun around, it was the realtor trying to get my attention. I stood there with my hand over my chest. "You scared me," I laughed.

"I'm sorry," she laughed with me. "We have ourselves a buyer. They want to go back to the office and process the paperwork."

"That's good news."

"They're offering $225,000 cash. It's $50,000 less than what you're asking, but I say run with it. What do you think?"

"Do they know what happened here?" I was curious.

"Yes, they are aware of it."

"Good. This is probably as good as it's going to get, so let's run it."

"Okay, let's do it."

I admired her perkiness and dedication to close on this deal, even though she was getting a nice commission check off of this. Mercedes was going to be happy to receive some good news finally, so I called her right away.

"Hello," she sniffled into the phone.

"Are you crying?" I asked.

"Yes."

"What's wrong?"

"It's bad, real bad," she cried.

My first thoughts were on my parents. "Is Mom and Dad okay?"

"They're fine. It's Nehiya."

In my mind, I couldn't care less about what was wrong with her. "Oh, what's going on with her?"

"She's dead. Two detectives came over and told us."

"What happened?"

"All they're saying is she was found dead off I-95."

I couldn't believe what I was hearing. Yes, I hated her with a passion because of the way she crossed me, but hearing she was thrown out like yesterday's trash made that old feeling go away and the hurt settle in.

"Damn, man. I hate to hear that happened to her."

"We're going down to the medical examiner's office." She hesitated for a second. "Are you coming?"

"Of course I am. I'm on my way right now. Text me the address."

"Okay, see you when you get here."

After hanging up the phone, I walked outside to stop Jill. "Hey, I have an emergency, and I have to go. I'll call you later."

"Is everything okay?" She tried reading my face. I could tell she was concerned.

"Someone close to me was found murdered." I started tearing up.

Jill stepped in and hugged me. "I'm so sorry for your loss, Barbee. You have my deepest sympathy. Is it someone I know?"

I paused for a second. "Nehiya." Jill and I crossed paths a few years ago, and we'd been cool ever since. Her dad owned the real estate company she works for.

She released me. "Wow. I'm truly sorry, and if you need anything, you let me know."

"Thank you."

When I got into the car, I adjusted my mirror and pulled out of the driveway. A horn blew loudly, causing me to slam on my brakes. I didn't see the car behind me as they sped by.

Mercedes' text message had just come through, so I plugged the address into my navigation system. I gave myself a minute to collect my thoughts before I backed all the way out this time. There was a Dodge Challenger parked on the side of the road as I headed up the street. It looked like Rich's car, but the tints were too dark. I also knew he wasn't aware of where I lived.

On the way there, I rode in silence. I needed time to think and process everything going on around me. It seemed like death was on every corner, along with the drama. These past few months were hell on earth, but before that everything was Gucci. If anyone told me six months ago I was going to endure so much pain, I would've called them a liar.

My tears started to flow heavily. Nehiya and I had been through so much and come so far together. I was starting to regret not talking to her. I knew she was back on drugs, and that was all the more reason to reach out to her and see what was going on. My pride got in the way of how I truly felt about her. Now I would never be able to make amends or apologize for outcasting her from the family. We were all she had, and now she was gone. She died all alone and probably in so much pain. I hoped and prayed she didn't suffer. Death had a funny way of making a person feel guilty about their actions.

When I stopped at a red light, I reached over to the glove box for a napkin to dry my eyes. My makeup was smeared and running down my face as I looked into the mirror at myself, but that was the least of my worries.

The Broward County Medical Examiner's Office was in Fort Lauderdale. It was a beige building, and as soon as I pulled into the parking lot next to Mercedes' car, butterflies invaded my stomach. My anxiety was at an all-time high. I tried using the breathing technique I learned from my anger management classes, but that shit wasn't working.

There was a tap on the window. I looked up and it was my dad, so I opened the car door and got out. "Hey, Papa."

His eyes were red from crying. I knew this was hard for him to do once again. First his very own daughter, then someone he considered a daughter. This was going to be hard for all of us.

"Hey, baby girl." He kissed my forehead. "How are you holding up?"

"It's hard, but I'll be okay."

My mom and Mercedes got out of the car and joined us. I hugged them both as well. "Hey, Mama." We just stood there embracing one another under the cool shade, because the sun was definitely out.

"Hey, baby. Are you going to be okay?" she asked while rubbing my back.

"Yes." I sniffled a little, trying to keep my tears in check before we went inside.

My father made the first move. "Come on, before I lose my nerve to go in here."

The building was cold as ice, and the smell of death lingered in the air, making me nauseous. We were escorted to the morgue. I swear it felt like I was walking the green mile down the well-lit hallway. Mercedes and I held hands until we stopped in front of a glass window. In the middle of the floor was a gleaming stainless steel table with a drain that held a lifeless body with a cotton white sheet over it. I clinched my chest tightly with my left hand and squeezed Mercedes' hand with the other to prepare myself for the sight coming soon.

"Give me one moment, and I will take you to the morgue. It's rare that we do this, but in this case we're making an exception," the M.E. informed us.

"Thanks, we appreciate this," my father responded.

The M.E. went inside, picked up some keys from the table, and returned to where we were standing. "Right this way."

We followed behind her closely once we made it inside the morgue, passing through a door that read 'Private.' Mercedes and I were still joined at the hip, nervous as if we were walking through some sort of haunted house.

"I'm going to give fair warning before I show you the body. Her body retained some fluid, so she's a little swollen, but her tattoos are still visible. We were able to preserve the body up until now because we couldn't reach a next of kin, until the detectives located you all."

.We stood in silence as she pulled the drawer open and removed the sheet. It was definitely Nehiya. There were bruises all over her naked body, and the tattoo of the broken heart on her thigh that read *Heart Breaker* was still there. My knees buckled and body shook. That same nauseous feeling returned, and I ran for the nearest trashcan. Vomit poured from my mouth due to the horrific sight before me.

"Is this her?" the M.E. asked.

"Yes," my father replied.

The medical examiner covered her up and pushed her back inside the cooler. "We have the jewelry she was wearing. The detectives bagged it as evidence once it was ruled a homicide." She then looked at me. "Are you okay?"

I nodded my head yes.

"What happened to her?" Mercedes asked.

"There was a single gunshot wound in her mouth that exited the back of her head. The bruising happened after she was already dead."

My father just stood there, shaking his head in disbelief.

In my mind, I knew whomever did this to Nehiya was trying to silence her. The problem was who was it, and why? There was no telling who did it because she could've been with anybody doing God knows what. The detective on the case didn't have any leads, so it became a cold case, and I knew we would probably never find out who her killer was. It could've easily been Meat, Giovanni, or any dude we robbed.

Deep down inside, my gut was telling me that Italian bastard was behind it. The detective told my parents she was murdered weeks ago and it was more than a coincidence it happened around the same time the shootout happened. If that was the case, I knew I needed to get rid of him A.S.A.P., because I was not giving him a second chance at killing me or someone else I loved.

We exited the building, and I went back to my car thinking of a master plan.

***

Rich

Seeing Barbee in such a delicate state made me weak for her, but I had to remember she was the enemy and crossed the line when she decided to set me up. She was walking out of the building with two women and one man. I assumed they were her parents, and I recognized her sister from the club the night we met.

Her mind had to be elsewhere, because there was one thing I knew about her: she was very observant. I had been watching Barbee at her old house when she was with the real estate agent. Apparently she received some bad news, because she was outside crying. What she didn't know was we made eye contact when she drove past my car after she almost hit another car backing out. I followed her to the medical examiner's office, and it made me wonder what she was there for.

The only thing that mattered now was where she lived at. I waited for her to pull out and hit the main road before I continued to follow her. There was no way I could risk blowing my cover.

"I got you now, baby. You won't get away this time," I mumbled under my breath.

There was something special about her that drew me in. If she would've chosen me instead of that nigga, she would've been in a much happier place. One thing I knew was I made this muthafuckin' world go 'round, and she would never find another nigga like me.

Barbee drove around town for an hour, and I was getting tired of following. She pulled up in the Publix parking lot and went inside. I parked in the row behind her so I could see her come out. While I waited, I fired up a cigarette. My cousin left his pack behind when we was sliding together, and that muthafucka came in handy. It was funny because I don't smoke, but dealing with a female like this made me do things I never considered doing.

Twenty minutes later, she returned to her car carrying a few grocery bags.

"Damn, bae, you cooking for this nigga, too? You ain't never made me shit, but all that's gonna change once we're back together."

Barbee got in the car and placed the bags next to her in the passenger seat. I knew she was going home after this. When she pulled off, I did the same, and we were back on the road again.

She traveled down Broward Boulevard going west and I was right there with her. She crossed over University Drive and made a right shortly after. Soon we were pulling up into an apartment complex. When she parked the car in her designated parking spot, she didn't get out immediately. That made me wonder if she saw me following her. I made sure to keep my distance, so I got out of the car and walked so I could see the apartment she was going in.

Not even a minute later, I saw some nigga walking outside toward her car, and she opened the door. I watched closely as she got out and gave him a kiss. That shit really made my fuckin' blood boil. If I wasn't in hiding, I would have blow up her spot and fucked that nigga up.

I waited until they went inside before I got back in my car and sped off.

Chapter 5

Barbee

"I'm taking Sierra to get her learner's permit today. Are you coming?" Corey asked as I lay in bed, trying to relax.

"No, I'm going to stay here and make some phone calls." I rolled on my side. "I have to make sure we're ready for the grand opening."

"Have you figured out a date yet?" He sat on the foot of the bed, putting on his shoes.

"Not yet, but we're pushing for the second week of summer."

"Why so far away?" he looked over at me.

"It's only a month away. This will give parents time to pay their rent and get their bad-ass kids situated," I joked.

Corey laughed. "That's a good point, babe."

"I know, right? I wanna make sure everyone is in the building when those doors open."

"It will be live, don't worry about that. All you need are some flyers and some bad bitches. The niggas gon' come. Females ain't spending money on strippers, no way."

"Oh yeah, I know that." By this time he was sitting up. I slid behind him and hugged him around his waist. "Don't you worry about the bad bitches."

"Why should I be worried? I have the bad bitch that owns the club."

I kissed his neck. "As long as you know what you have."

"I definitely know that," Corey smiled.

"Good." I slid from behind him and stood up. "Now, go take Sierra before I make y'all late."

Corey knew what I meant by that. "I don't mind being late," he smirked.

"Sierra does, now get up." I pulled him up by his arms and hugged him. Corey did the same and planted a kiss on my lips.

"Keep it warm for me." He smacked me on the ass and walked out of the room.

"I will."

Sierra was still in her bedroom with the door closed, so he knocked. "Let's go, Sierra, before I change my mind."

He knew damn well that wasn't gon' happen, especially since she was pregnant and was going to need transportation once the baby arrived. We both had busy schedules, and when the club opened in June, I wouldn't have time to chauffer her around.

Dre agreed to help pay for her car after she got her license. Since our meeting, he had really stepped up. He even took her to her first doctor's appointment. I was supposed to take her, but I knew him doing that would make her happy to see him involved. Now, as far as Tokee went, I had no clue if she knew or if she was in the dark about it, but that wasn't my business. Hell, I had my own issues. As long as she didn't put her hands on Sierra or cause problems, I was cool with it. She knew what she was dealing with for the next 18 years, which is why I advised her to think hard about it, because it wasn't going to be easy.

"I'm ready," Sierra said as she emerged from her bedroom with a huge smile on her face.

"I knew that would bring you out of there," said Corey.

"You just looking for an excuse to not take me, but we're going, so let's go." She grabbed his hand and escorted him to the front door.

"I'll walk y'all out," I replied while grabbing my keys from the key holder mounted on the wall. We walked outside, and I closed the door behind us.

Corey looked over his shoulder at me. "Did you lock the door?"

"No. I'm coming right back. I'm just checking the mailbox before I go back in." I continued to walk behind him.

"Just checking, 'cause I don't need nobody trying to kidnap my wife," he laughed.

"You so crazy." I stopped in my tracks. "See y'all later, and good luck on your test."

"Thanks, sis."

After watching Corey and Sierra pull off, I headed to my destination. Standing in front of the box, I unlocked it and pulled the door open. There was mainly junk mail with the exception of the light bill. I hated that shit 'cause they will pack a mailbox with everything except for coupons for Popeye's.

"Ain't that a bitch." I mumbled under my breath.

When I closed the door, I took a step back and bumped into a warm body. I nearly jumped out of my skin. Standing in front of me was this strange man I always saw in passing or in the parking lot of the complex. He was always staring at me, and it made me feel uncomfortable, so I took a step back.

"Hello, beautiful," he smiled.

"Hi." I eased away so I could leave quickly.

"Have a nice day."

"You too."

I swear I did the 100-yard dash when I hit the corner, all the way back to the apartment. The door was unlocked, so I ran inside and locked the door behind me. When I turned around, I took a deep breath, relieved I was no longer in his presence.

Looking up, I realized my biggest threat was already in my home, sitting on my sofa. The mail I had clutched in my hand slipped from my grip and onto the floor. My heart rate sped up tremendously, and I could not utter a single word. This could not be happening to me right now.

"Surprised to see me, baby?" he grinned.

"Wha–what are you doing here?" I stuttered, which was something I never did, but shit, I was scared of this crazy bastard and didn't have a gun near me.

"I told you that you would be seeing me soon." Rich stood up and rubbed his hands together. "I came to get what belongs to me."

I backed up toward the door so I could unlock it, but he was quick on his feet when he rushed me. He placed his hand on the door.

"Where you think you going?"

"I don't have anything that belongs to you." I had to test him and see what he was talking about. As far as I knew, he could've been talking about the product we stole from Giovanni, his connect.

"You belong to me," he nodded toward the room, "so go get your things and let's go. You coming with me."

"I'm not going anywhere with you, so you need to leave." I had to show him I wasn't afraid of him and he had no authority over me.

"Not without you, I'm not." He raised his hand at me, causing me to flinch. Then he stroked my cheek with his finger. "Why you jumping? I'm not going to hurt you. I love you, Barbee."

I moved my head to the side to avoid his touch, but his hands followed. "Rich, you don't love me," I whispered.

That soft, warm look in his eyes disappeared, and they suddenly became dark and cold. I knew I made him angry.

"Don't tell me how I feel, because you don't know." At this point he was belligerent. He put his finger in my face. "You have no idea how I feel about you."

Specks of spit flew from his mouth and landed on my face with every word he enunciated. I was disgusted, but I didn't attempt to wipe my face. I just stood there. All I wanted was for him to leave, but something was telling me this wasn't going to be easy.

"Rich, how did you find me?" I was almost scared to ask, but I needed to know where this psycho got his info from.

"I followed you home one day." This nigga smiled like there was nothing wrong with stalking.

"What?" That shit threw me for a loop because I didn't see how that was possible. We didn't run in the same circles, and we didn't know the same people.

"Did you sell your house?" he asked.

"How do you know about my house?"

"I saw you talking to your realtor."

Rich tried to kiss me, but I moved my head once more. Feeling his lips on my neck made my skin crawl. "Rich, stop, please," I begged.

He ignored me and kissed me again. His hands crept up my thigh, all the way up to my ass. "I saw you crying that day." He paused and shook his head. "I wanted to get out the car and comfort you, but I knew you would've rejected me. I even followed you to the medical examiner's office."

That was confirmation he wasn't lying. This man followed me and watched me for hours without me noticing him at all. I had a feeling I saw his car, but I brushed it off. Now I saw I was right all along.

"So, who is this nigga you living with?"

"Huh?"

"You heard me. Who is this nigga?"

I played dumb. "I don't know what you're talking about."

"Don't lie to me, 'cause I saw y'all in the parking lot hugging and shit."

The bass in his voice made me jump a little. I had been fucking with a loose cannon all along and never knew it. "Rich, I need you to leave before my boyfriend gets back."

"I'm not leaving without you, so let's go, and I'm not gon' keep saying the same thing."

"I can't go with you," I pleaded, but he just wasn't getting it.

Rich placed his hand on his head like I was giving his crazy-ass a headache or he was in deep thought. "Barbee, I'm trying to be patient with you, but you are making this harder than it needs to be, and it's pissing me off." He paused for a second, waiting on me to move, but when I stood in place, it pissed him off even more. "Go pack your shit," he screamed.

I watched him closely as he reached into his waistband. I wasn't slow by a long shot, so I knew he was about to pull out a gun. My first instinct sent me running down the hallway full-speed into our bedroom. I tried closing the door, but he had his foot in the way.

"Rich, just leave me alone, please."

My back was against the door, using every muscle in my body to keep him out. I reached for my cellphone that was on the dresser next to the bedroom door. I dialed Corey's number, but before he could answer, Rich burst through the door, knocking me to the floor. My cellphone slid under the bed. This nigga was like the Incredible Hulk or some shit. I crawled backward on the floor, trying to get away like one of those white girls from a scary movie.

"Stop resisting me." Rich picked me up from the floor, threw me onto the bed, and climbed on top of me. His gun was still in his hand, so I was trying not to make any sudden movements to make it go off. Tears finally pricked my eyes once I realized I was in more danger than I originally thought I was. It took a lot for me to cry, and that moment presented itself again.

Rich rubbed the barrel of the gun against my breasts and all the way down to my navel.

"Rich, please," I muttered.

"Just relax, baby. I'm not gon' hurt you."

"Don't do this, please." I was panting as he continued to caress my body against my will.

Suddenly he grew irritated with my cries and snatched me up from the bed by my arm.

"Ow!" He squeezed my arm tight. My mind was telling me to try to grab his gun, but I was afraid he would probably shoot me.

"Be quiet, and let's go. I'm done playing with you."

"No, please."

I tried to run into the bathroom, but he grabbed me and there was a tussle. In the midst of it all he dropped his gun. I tried to fight him, but he was too strong. We were knocking things off the dresser. We even cracked the mirror when he pushed me against it. He picked up his gun from the floor and aimed it at me.

"You have two choices. You can come with me voluntarily or involuntarily. The choice is yours."

I walked down the hallway in silence, trying to think of a way to get out of this mess, but I kept drawing a blank.

A sudden hit to the back of my head caused me stumble and hit the floor.

***

Corey

I was flying down Broward Boulevard, trying to get home as quickly as possible. I must've run every light on the way there. All I knew was in the next hour I would probably be in jail for a double homicide. While I sat in the car waiting on Sierra to take her test, I received a call from Barbee. When I answered, she didn't say anything, and I told her before to put a lock on her phone so she would stop dialing me by accident. I guess she never did it.

Just before I decided to hang up, I could hear moaning in the background and the sound of a nigga. If this bitch was fucking a nigga in my shit, she just committed suicide, and that was a promise.

All I could hear in my mind over and over again was her voice saying, *"Rich, please."* Then his voice: *"Just relax, baby, I'm not gon' hurt you."*

This muthafucka had me fucked up if she thought she was about to get away with this shit. I was about to surprise her ass. No wonder she didn't want to come with us. She wanted to be laid up with the next nigga, getting fucked in my crib. This ho didn't have the decency to go to a hotel and cheat, or to the nigga's house.

"Get the fuck out the way," I shouted at the car in front of me. This bitch was moving like we was in a muthafuckin' funeral line. I swerved around her and gunned it until I hit Jacaranda.

Once I made it to my parking spot, I shut the car off and ran to my apartment. I slid the key in slowly and carefully to make sure they couldn't hear me, but the top wasn't locked. I twisted the bottom, and that was unlocked, too. When I walked inside, I closed the door gently.

The first thing I noticed was the mail on the floor. It was too quiet for anyone to be in there, so I made my way down the hallway and to the bedroom. There was no one there. What I noticed was my room was trashed, the mirror was broken, and the bed was a mess. Something didn't feel right about the scene before me.

I pulled my cellphone out and called her. When I heard her phone ringing, my heart skipped a beat. I got down on my knees and looked under the bed, and there it was. I picked the phone up and tried to check her call log, but there was a lock code on it. Now my mind was really fucked up because it made no sense. If her phone was locked, that meant she didn't call me by accident, and it was meant for me to hear. The only thing now was why would she want me to hear that?

"Come on, Corey, use your head. This your girl you talking about, and you know her. She wouldn't do no shit like that."

After talking to myself for a few minutes, I remembered she told me one of the residents was always watching her, and it made her nervous. I grabbed my gun and headed out the door to his apartment. He lived in the building behind us.

I banged on his door, and when he opened it, he staring into the barrel of my pistol. I didn't give that nigga a chance to speak. "Where the fuck is my wife, nigga?"

"I don't know." His eyes were wide as flying saucers.

"Don't play games with me. Back the fuck up." He did as he was told. "Who in here with you?" I shut the door behind me.

"Nobody. Go and look."

I pushed him. "Let's go." Every room was searched thoroughly. I even checked that nigga's cabinets, and there was no sign of her or a struggle. "Have you seen her today?"

He nodded his head yes. "Earlier, at the mailbox, and that's it. I swear." He seemed sincere, but he was a suspect until I found my girl, and I meant that shit.

"Did you see her leave with anybody?"

"No. I came back in here after that."

"You better be telling the truth, or when I see you again, you a dead man."

Tucking my pistol away, I left his apartment and hit Amon up. "What's up, bruh?" There was a lot of noise in his background.

"I can't find Barbee, man."

"Y'all, shut the fuck up. I can't hear." The noise stopped immediately. "Now, what you was saying? You can't find Barbee?"

"Nah. I took Sierra to the DMV and I got a call from her, but she wasn't saying nothing. I just heard noise in the background. I rushed home to see what was going on, and it looks like there was a struggle in this bitch."

"That shit don't sound right."

"Something happened to her. She left her cell, keys, and her purse. Nothing is missing."

Amon was silent for a moment. "You don't think that Italian dude got her?"

"Ain't no telling, man. We gotta find my baby, bruh."

"Stay put. I'm on my way to you."

"Hurry up."

"I'm leaving now."

When I got back inside, I plopped down on the couch and held my head. I couldn't fathom losing her. My thoughts went back to the day she was shot and I thought I lost her for good. Now I was feeling like it was happening again. Whoever had her was going to die, and I put that on the child we lost. Barbee was my world, and I needed her in it. She made me feel complete, and I couldn't imagine me being happy in life without her.

"Ugh!" I screamed.

I took her phone out my pocket and tried to crack the code, but I couldn't get it right. Giving up was not an option, so I kept trying until I locked myself out completely. Frustrated, I threw the phone across the room. This was when I needed to keep my head on straight and figure out my next move, but I couldn't because I didn't know if she was dead or being tortured. A drink was what I needed to calm me down, so I went into the kitchen and grabbed the Patron I bought a few days ago. Popping the top off, I took a big gulp and sat it on the table.

By the time Amon got there, I was almost finished with the bottle. He walked inside and went into the room to take a look.

"Oh yeah, somebody took her. Ain't no doubt in my mind about that." He looked at me. "We're gonna find her. Where is her phone?"

"It's locked. I tried to get in it and see who the last person she talked to was, but I can't figure out her code."

"Grab the phone. I know this geeky-ass nigga who specialize in that shit. Did you call the police?"

"Nah."

"Good. We gon' take care of this shit on our own. I know that nigga had something to do with this. The only thing is, how did he find her?"

"I don't know man."

Amon and I left the apartment in a hurry. Time was ticking, and we had none to waste. When we got to his car, he made a phone call.

"Hey, Josh. This Amon."

"What's up, woe?"

"I got a phone I need you to get into for me."

"I'm at the crib. Come through."

"I'm on the way."

We drove out to Davie by the Broward College Campus. I was surprised to see Josh was a geeky black kid. I was expecting a white kid with freckles. That showed how stereotypical we could be, but as far as I was concerned, this li'l nigga could've been purple. As long as he unlocked the phone, I didn't give a fuck.

"Josh, this my brother, Corey."

"What's up, man?" said Josh.

"Nothing much." We shook hands and he escorted us to his work area.

"Where's the phone?"

I pulled it from my pocket, and that's when I noticed the screen on the bitch was cracked. "Fuck!" I shouted.

"What's wrong?" Amon asked.

"I broke the bitch when I threw it in the house."

"Let me see." Josh took a look at it. "I can hack the phone, but I'm going to need some time."

"How much time?" Amon asked.

"A few days."

I knew it was my fault, but I wasn't going for that answer. "We don't have a few days. Time is precious. I'll pay you whatever, but I needed this done, like, two hours ago."

"I'll see what I can do."

Amon placed his hand on his shoulder. "It's an emergency, so I need your word you'll move fast. My cousin was kidnapped, and I don't know how much time she has left."

"I'll get started right now, and soon as I crack it, I'll call you."

"That sounds better," Amon replied.

"I need all text messages and the call log," I added.

"I'm on it."

We left because there was nothing else we could do besides wait, and that was sure to have me on pins and needles. My phone rang, and I was hoping it was Barbee, but it wasn't. It was Sierra. I looked at Amon.

"Take me the DMV to pick up my sister. I almost forgot about her."

Destiny Skai

Chapter 6

Barbee

I woke up in a hot-ass basement and looked around, but for the life of me I couldn't figure out how in the hell I ended up there. I was a little disoriented, but I couldn't figure out why. When I looked down, I realized I was tied to a chair with duct tape over my mouth. I closed my eyes and opened them to wake up from the horrible dream. I tried it one more time, but the scenery never changed. The restraints were so tight I couldn't wiggle myself free. I was secured to the max.

Suddenly, I heard the basement door open, then the creaking from the stairs. It was creepy, like something from a scary movie. Then there was a familiar voice. For the first time in a long time, I started praying to God for help. When I saw Rich's face, I panicked and tried to break free.

"Barbee!" Mercedes screeched. She rushed over to me and took the duct tape off my mouth. "What happened?" she asked. She then reached out to untie me.

There was a click from a gun. "I wouldn't do that, sweetheart, if I were you." We looked up and saw Rich had the gun pointed at us.

"What are you doing, Rich?" Mercedes asked.

"Holding up my end of the deal. It's called loyalty, but you wouldn't know nothing about that, would you, Barbee?" He looked at Mercedes. "Sit in that chair next to her." She did what she was told, and he tied her up as well.

"What end of the deal you talking about?" I asked out of curiosity.

Rich laughed, and it was wicked. "I made a deal with the devil himself, and I must say the payoff was quite nice." He could tell we were confused. "Don't worry so much. You will

have a chance to ask all the questions you want in due time."
His phone rang, cutting him off. "Hello."

There was a long pause. Whomever he was speaking to was long-winded. I could hear him talking, but I couldn't understand what he was saying.

"As soon as I get her, I will deliver her to you personally." Then he hung up the phone.

"Who was that?" I asked.

"The devil," he snapped. "Didn't I just say you will get to ask questions?"

Something told me it was Giovanni, but I needed him to confirm it. "Why did you bring my sister here? I thought you only wanted me."

"Leverage," he responded.

"Leverage for what?"

"Let's just cut to the chase. Did you rob Giovanni?"

I knew that's what this was about. He had finally told him what happened. I wasn't sure how to answer, although his demeanor was cool.

"What's wrong, Barbee? Cat gotcha tongue, or did you leave it in that nigga's boxers?" Rich laughed at his joke. "I have a question for you. Did you ever feel anything for me, or were you playing me all along?"

"No, I wasn't playing you." I dropped my head. "Things just didn't work out as planned."

"Did you rob Giovanni?" Rich asked again, but I didn't answer him. He drew his weapon and aimed it at Mercedes. "You better start talking, or I'm gonna put a bullet in her head.

I couldn't risk him shooting her, so I sang like a bird. Shit, it wasn't like he didn't know already. "Yes, I did. But she had nothing to do with it, so let her go. I'll tell you everything."

"Do I look stupid to you? Let her go so she could call the police? Nope, she's staying right here with you." He lowered his gun. "Continue with the story, or I'm gonna do her like Giovanni did Nehiya."

"What?" My assumption was dead-on. I knew he was behind her death. "What do you know about her death?"

"I know she snitched about the whole operation, and he put a bullet in her mouth. Do you want that to happen to her?"

Mercedes didn't say a word. She just watched him closely.

Rich then pointed the gun at me, so I started to cry. "Rich, don't do this, please. I'll tell you everything. I swear." This was my chance to earn his trust. "When I met you in the club, you were my intended target."

He cut me off immediately. "For what?"

"I robbed dudes for a living, and that's why I said you didn't want a female like me. But I don't do that anymore." Rich nodded his head. "The plan was to rob you, but then I started to fall for you."

"Bullshit," he shouted.

"It's the truth, Rich. She told us we couldn't rob you anymore," Mercedes jumped in.

"The plan was dead at that moment, but then you took me to Giovanni's house, and that's when I put a plan into motion to rob him instead. After that, everything was smooth until I fell out with Nehiya, and that's when she blew the whistle on everything." I wasn't sure if that's what she did, but I knew he would buy it. "After that, he sent his shooters to my house to kill us, but he–he," I paused. Talking about Chyna's death was making me emotional. "They killed my sister and our unborn baby, Rich. They shot me, too." Tears fell from my eyes as I went over those horrible events once again.

Rich suddenly lost his balance, stumbled to a chair, and sat down. "What baby?"

"Our baby," I lied. "I was pregnant at the time, and that's why I pulled back from you. We were so fresh in our relationship, and I didn't know what to do."

"How do I know that wasn't that nigga's baby?" He looked up through hooded eyes, like he didn't believe me.

"I was only sleeping with you at the time. He was nowhere in the picture."

"Giovanni killed our baby?"

I guess he needed reassurance, and I was more than happy to give it to him. "Yes. He ruined our chance to be a family." I could see the anger in his eyes, and I knew I had gotten to him. "After that, I never wanted to see you again."

Rich sat and thought for a minute before he approached me slowly. I wasn't sure what he was about to do. I hoped he bought the pregnancy story and was having a change of heart.

The closer he got, the harder my heart beat. Rubbing his fingers through my hair, he whispered in my ear, "I'm sorry you had to go through that, but I'm here now, and you have nothing to worry about. We'll make another baby."

That was not the answer I was looking for, but I guessed it would have to do for now. "Okay. Are you going to let me go? I promise not to run or resist you." Here I was lying again, but I knew he had a weak spot for me.

Rich grinned. "Barbee, we got trust issues, and we have to work on that before we go any further. What I will do is put the gun away, and I promise not to pull it out on you or your sister as long as you keep your word."

"Okay, I can do that."

Rich bent down in front of me and kissed me. I kissed him back, but of course there was no passion there. That fire died a long time ago. I was in survival mode, and I was going to do everything in my power to keep us alive.

"Damn, I've missed kissing you." He grabbed his crotch and licked his lips. "Someone else misses you, too. How about we get reacquainted upstairs?"

"Okay."

While Rich untied me from the chair, Mercedes was shaking her head no. *Don't do it,* she mouthed to me.

It's okay, I responded. We could read lips very well.

Rich grabbed my arm and helped me up from the chair, but my hands were still tied. I followed him upstairs and through the kitchen until we came across a bedroom. The house was wooden and old, yet in immaculate shape. The bedroom was decorated in floral prints like it belonged to old people. The dressers were solid brown, and so was the bed. This décor was definitely from the sixties.

"Whose house is this?" I continued to look around the room, trying not to make eye contact with him.

"It was my grandparents' house. It's been in the family for years, and I've kept it up ever since they died many years ago."

Rich faced me and placed the gun inside the dresser drawer. Our lips touched once more, and his hands found their way to my breast. He removed his jeans and his boxers before pushing me onto the bed.

"Untie me." Rich removed the bungee cord from my wrists and tossed it on the floor.

Climbing on top of me, he pushed my dress up to my waist. I wasn't wearing any panties, so the access was easy. As he thrust himself inside of me, I closed my eyes and imagined I was someplace else.

I was living with Meat at 16 years old. In the beginning, all we did was fuck like rabbits. He taught me how to suck dick and take it in every hole. This dude had my mind blown because he did shit to my body I didn't think could be done. My nose was wide open, and I would fight every female I thought wanted him or looked at him the wrong way. After a while, they stopped giving him attention and would look the other way when we were together.

Six months down the line was when things started to change, and suddenly I was doing things a wife would do. He had me cooking and cleaning and washing his clothes. The rules had changed, and he even gave me a curfew, but I wasn't going for that shit. So, one night I came in the house late on purpose, and he was pissed.

"Where the fuck have you been? I've been sitting here waiting on you." He was sitting on the couch in the dark.

"I was hanging out with my friends."

"I told you to be home by 10." He stood up in front of me.

"I know, but the time slipped me by."

Meat cocked back and hit me in the face so hard I hit the floor. My nose was bleeding. He looked down at me with no remorse.

"Get up and go clean yourself up, and the next time I tell you something, you better listen." He paused for a second. "And tomorrow you better not leave this house, or the day after that. As a matter of fact, don't leave here without permission."

I sat on the floor crying because I couldn't believe he hit me, but I guess I was taking too long. Meat grabbed me by my arms and dragged me into the bathroom.

I stood up under the water and took a long, hot shower and cried. When I finally came out, he was sitting on the bed waiting for me, but I ignored him. I climbed in on my side of the bed and tried to fall asleep. A few minutes later, he was cuddled up behind me.

"I'm sorry I hit you." I didn't say anything. "I won't do it again, I promise." The tears were falling easily, but I didn't move a muscle, let alone say a word. He kissed me on the

cheek and apologized again. Meat grabbed me by the shoulders and rolled me onto my back. That night was the first night he made love to me. He even cried in the process.

Needless to say, I forgave him for hitting me.

My time travel to the past was cut abruptly due to the sound of Rich moaning. "Hmm! This pussy so good. It's still tight. That nigga can't be laying the dick like me," he boasted.

Every time he stroked my inner core, I bit down on my lip to keep any sound from creeping through. All I wanted was for it to be over. His hands slipped underneath my butt cheeks, pushing me upward so my pelvis could meet his thrusts. Our bodies were sweaty, and the sounds of skin slapping filled the room, yet I remained silent. The thickness of his penis opened me up, and my vaginal walls adjusted to his girth and my juices began to flow freely. I repeated in my head, *this is not for enjoyment, this is not for enjoyment.* No matter how much I told myself that, my body was singing a different tune. Seconds later, I was gushing all over him.

Rich continued to fuck me hard until he came inside of me. I wished he would've worn a condom instead of leaving his semen behind, but this would be the last time he fucked me.

After he busted his nut, he lay down beside me on his back, breathing hard. I closed my eyes, pretending I was going to sleep. Thirty minutes later, he was sound asleep.

I crept from the bed slowly, making sure I didn't awake him in the process. Tip-toeing from the room, I eased my way back down to the basement.

"Barbee, are you okay?" Mercedes asked when she saw my face.

"Sh! We have to get out of here now." I untied her hands first, and then I went for the chair.

"I wouldn't do that if I were you," Rich said as he made his way down the stairs. He was really calm. "If you look underneath the chair, you will see a bomb. And if she gets up, it will detonate."

There was no way he did all of that. I just wasn't convinced he would go through all of that trouble, but then again, this was Rich we were talking about. Easing down onto the floor, I looked under the chair, and lo and behold, there was a compact black box with a flashing green light. My eyes grew wide.

This nigga is really trying to kill me!

***

Corey

It had been 18 hours since we dropped the phone off to Josh. My patience was growing thinner by the second. I didn't get any sleep worrying about my wife and what type of pain she could possibly be enduring. Amon and I sat in my living room trying to come up with a plan on how to get her back. We weren't one hundred percent certain about who took her, but we had a pretty good idea it was Giovanni. He was the only person I could think of, especially with the tragedy he caused a few months ago. I knew Barbee wanted revenge for her sister's death, but I told her to let that go because I would handle it when the time was right. I couldn't approach someone like that without a plan. This man had security, not the average drug dealer, so we needed to proceed with caution. I just hoped she didn't initiate and go against what I instructed her not to do.

Amon's phone rang, and my heart skipped a beat. I prayed it was good news. He put the phone on speaker.

"Tell me something good."

"I can tell you something great. Well, not so great, but I think I have some information that could be helpful in locating your cousin."

"And what's that?" I asked.

"Come by the house and I'll show you. I'm sure you don't want to discuss this over the phone."

"We on the way," Amon said while picking up his keys and heading to the door.

Amon flushed it to Davie. We were both filled with the anticipation of not knowing what to expect with the results. I just wanted my baby back in one piece.

"Did Barbee ever tell you how she met this dude in the first place?" I asked.

He hesitated. "Nah."

For some odd reason I got the feeling he wasn't being truthful with me, so I turned toward him so I could look in his eyes. "You don't sound too sure about that. What's the deal, man?"

Amon closed his eyes for a split second and shook his head. "A'ight. This dude she was kicking it with introduced her to Giovanni."

"She was fucking this nigga?" There was no need to beat around the bush, so I got straight to the point of what I wanted to know. "The same nigga I suspected she was cheating with, and you knew about it?"

"Nah, man, chill. I don't know the depth of their relationship. All I know is she was setting up this nigga name Rich, so she had to get close to him. Shit, when she was close enough, he took her when he conducted his business."

Now I was hot and worried at the same damn time. "She fucked that nigga, and you can't tell me she didn't. Ain't no nigga taking a chick he ain't fucking to meet his connect."

"Listen, I'm telling you what I know. You have to ask her that when we get her back."

For the duration of the ride I just sat back and thought about the time I caught her. I knew she fucked somebody that same day because I could feel the difference. I knew I was packing and could do some damage, so that meant the nigga she fucked was ruined if I could feel it. Barbee had me so mad, but I knew I had to shake it off in order for me to find her. If I didn't go into this thing with a strong head, I could fuck it up for all of us. All I knew was she had some explaining to do when her ass was safe. I was prepared to do whatever it took to get her back home.

I put Sierra up in a hotel and paid one of my boys to keep an eye on her until this shit was over. There was no telling who was watching my place, so until I had this shit under wraps, my place was off limits.

We pulled up into the complex and got out of the car quickly. Josh was standing at the door, waiting on us.

"That was quick."

"Yeah, my cousin's life is on the line," Amon replied, walking past him.

"Well, I found some info that will be quite helpful in locating her."

"That's what we wanna hear."

Josh sat down at his workstation and passed us some papers. "These are some text messages between her and – I'm assuming – a man. I must warn you, though, they are not pleasant at all."

I scanned the messages, and the ones that caught my attention were the ones that had recently happened.

4:42 p.m.
You fucked with the wrong one, and you'll see me soon. I love you, Barbee, how could you do this to me. All I wanted to do was to give you everything your heart desires, and you would shit on me like

that? You are a heartless and cruel bitch!! I hate you.

4:44 p.m.
I'm sorry, bae, I didn't mean any of that. I love you!

Reading these messages confirmed what I already knew: she fucked this nigga. If this number belonged to the infamous Rich, then he had her, and all we had to do was figure out where to find him. Hopefully we could get an address.

"Can you find out who the phone number belongs to?" I asked Josh.

"I'm two steps ahead of you. The phone is listed under a Michelle Gathers, and this is the address." Josh handed me the piece of paper with the details on it. "There's also another address listed among the text messages. That may be helpful as well."

"You're a genius." Amon placed his hand on Josh's shoulder. "I really appreciate the quick turn around." He reached into his pocket and handed him some cash. "It's a stack."

"No problem." Josh placed the money into his desk drawer.

"You're not going to count it?" Amon asked.

"If I have to count it, then that means I don't trust you," Josh replied.

"I guess you're right about that." Amon stood up. "You ready?"

"Yeah." I stood up and shook hands with Josh. "Thanks, man."

"I hope you find your girl." Josh escorted us to the door, and we were on our way to find Barbee. "Hold up. I have something y'all might need." Josh returned quickly with a bag. "But you didn't get this from me though."

"You already know." Amon grabbed the bag and we were on our way.

Chapter 7

Barbee

That was a close call. If he would've stayed inside a few seconds longer, Mercedes and I would've been dead. I really didn't believe he was this crafty or crazy to actually put a bomb in a chair to keep me hostage. After that little stunt I pulled, I knew he wasn't going to trust me anymore. I sat back down in the chair and looked him dead in the eyes.

"I'm sorry for what I did, but could you just let my sister go? She has nothing to do with this."

"You're not in a position to ask for favors. You're not good on keeping your word."

"I just wanted her to get away. I'll stay here willingly."

"I don't believe anything that comes from your pretty, little, lying lips."

"Rich, she has nothing to do with this. Just please, let her go."

My pleas fell on deaf ears because he didn't acknowledge any of my begging, and that was something I didn't do, but my sister's life was on the line. I cared more about her safety than my own.

"I'll be leaving here soon, and I want you to be on your best behavior." He smirked, and it made my skin crawl.

"I will. I promise."

Rich picked up his phone and made a call. "Hey, fam, I need you out here at the bunny ranch," he laughed.

"Bunny ranch," I repeated to myself. This was one twisted dude, and he was happy about it.

Mercedes looked at me, shaking her head.

"I'm sorry," I whispered.

"I know. We're gonna get out of here."

Just then Rich hung up the phone. "I know you didn't think I was leaving you here all alone. Trust goes a long way, and since we don't have that, I had to get y'all a babysitter." He walked over to me and tied me up to the chair once again, but this time not as harshly.

We sat around in suspense for an hour just waiting to see who was going to show up. Finally, Rich's cellphone sent a notification. I assumed that was what he was waiting on, because he got up and left the room without a word. Minutes later we could hear the creaking noise from the steps, and behind him stood a tall, dark-skinned dude with dreads and golds.

"You a wild-ass nigga," he said to Rich. "You got you two baddies down here, boy."

"Yeah, I know. This one here," Rich pointed at me, "she did ya' boy dirty, and unfortunately her sister has to suffer the consequences with her. I have to go on a mission, so I need you to sit here for a few hours. Keep an eye on her, she's a sneaky one. I already advised her there's a bomb underneath the chair, so if she gets up, *kaboom!*" he shouted.

"What if she has to pee?" I asked Rich.

"She can pee in the chair."

"That's gross, Rich, don't do that."

"You ruined it for her, sweetie." He walked away and went about his business, leaving us alone with a stranger.

I waited twenty minutes before I tried the dark, handsome fella. "Can you take me to the bathroom, please?"

"Nah, I can't do that, sweetie. You heard the man." He smiled and displayed the sexiest set of dimples I had ever seen.

"He said my sister couldn't get up, but not me."

"Just relax and try not to think about it."

"You would let my sister pee on herself?" Mercedes asked. "I know you're not as sick as your friend."

"Listen, cutie pies, I came to do one job, and one job only, and that's to babysit. Nothing more, nothing less."

"Come on, please? You have the gun. Do you really think I would jeopardize getting me or my sister killed?"

He thought long and hard about it before he finally got up to approach me. "Listen, you have thirty seconds to use the bathroom, and if you try anything, I will shoot you. And that's a promise."

"Okay, I won't." He untied me from the chair.

"I'll follow you."

I made my way up the stairs, and he directed me straight to the bathroom. That was clarification in my eyes that this was not his first time here. It also made me wonder how many times they had held people captive in this home. I turned to face him with my hands out.

"Can you loosen this for me, please?"

"Nice try."

"How do you expect me to wipe myself?"

"I can think of a few ways."

The look in his eyes told me I didn't want to find out what my other options were. "Never mind." I stepped inside, closed the door, and locked it behind me. I knew he was listening, so I turned on the water to throw him off. I rummaged through the medicine cabinet looking for any type of weapon I could find, but to no avail. Moving quickly, I searched through the bottom cabinet. The only things I saw were prescription bags from Walgreen's for none other than Richard Gathers. I couldn't believe what I was reading, but it shed light on why he was so crazy in the first place. According to the medication pamphlet, Rich was taking antipsychotic pills.

There was a knock on the door. "Hurry up. It doesn't take that long to pee."

Closing the cabinets gently, I stood to my feet and shut off the water before opening the door.

***

Rich

Barbee had my blood boiling. I walked through the door of my home and slammed the door.

"What the hell is wrong with you?" Michelle snapped.

I bypassed her and continued to make my way to our bedroom, but that didn't stop her from following me because she was directly on my heels.

"I asked you a question, so you need to answer me."

"Nothing." Turning my head, I avoided looking in her direction. She knew I was lying, but she wasn't about to get the truth from me.

"So, you're slamming doors for nothing?"

"I thought you were doing something?"

"I was until you stepped in here, mad at the world."

If Michelle even caught a whiff of the truth, she would've left me at the drop of a dime. The truth was I was married and had been for nine years now, but I never told Barbee. I'd been living a double life for the past six months, which is why I had the condo. Michelle had no idea I purchased it a year ago, and I planned on keeping it that way.

"Well, I didn't ask you to come in here, so can you go back into the other room?" It wasn't exactly a question. I was telling her exactly what she needed to do in order to keep the peace.

Michelle began to walk away, but she stopped in her tracks and turned around to face me. Standing in front of me, she put her finger in my face. "Don't come in here with an attitude because one of your many hos made you mad."

I sucked my teeth. I was not in the mood for her bickering. "Man, get the fuck out of here with that bullshit," I yelled.

"And what are you going to do?"

See, I was up on her game, and I was trying to keep calm and avoid a terrible situation. Instead of entertaining her, I walked away and headed in the direction of the bathroom, but before I could get inside and close the door, she pushed my head.

"I know you started back fucking somebody," she shouted.

"Whatever, and stop following me, because you being real childish right now."

"Fuck you! You're the one out here fucking these nasty-ass hos." She was making the situation worse by the second, but I knew she didn't care. Every day she sat in the house because I kept her on a tight leash. She didn't do anything outside of the house unless I was there. I knew Michelle was tired of her repetitive schedule and was craving my attention, but now wasn't the time.

"If you know all of this, then tell me why the fuck you still here?" I grinned, testing her patience.

"I don't know. Maybe I should go back to where I came from." I knew I hit a nerve because her expression told it all. "'Cause apparently you haven't changed."

As soon as I turned my back to her, Michelle grabbed the remote control and hit me in the back of the head with it. My reaction was quick, and she didn't see it coming. I slapped her so hard she lost her balance, but she didn't fall. I was so upset I didn't bother to see if she was okay, and at that moment I really didn't care. Michelle stood there slack-jawed because she never expected that outcome. She had finally gotten what she was looking for, and now she didn't know what to do.

"I hope you're satisfied."

"Fuck you! Real men don't hit women."

That made me snicker, because she had lost her rabbit-ass mind. "Start acting like one instead of a little-ass girl and I would treat you like one."

"Fuck you, pussy-ass nigga."

Michelle had officially crossed the line, and she knew it because she started to back up slowly.

"What was that?" I needed to be sure I heard her correctly, but she didn't respond. "Repeat what you just said to me." If she had any street knowledge, she would've known there was one thing to never call a man, and that was it. She should've spit in my face for that matter, because that was exactly what it felt like.

"You heard me."

I knew she wasn't about to repeat herself. The veins in my forehead and neck were clearly visible, and she knew exactly what that meant. She knew she went way beyond her boundaries, and it was about to get ugly.

I walked up to her and grabbed her by her hair. "Now, repeat what you just said."

"Rich, let go of my hair, and I'm not playing with you," she demanded.

"What the fuck you gon' do? You think because you pregnant you can talk to me sideways? Bitch, your face ain't pregnant."

Michelle's posture was stiff as a board. The problem was she was used to throwing temper tantrums and getting her way, but that shit wasn't working today. Barbee had already pissed me the fuck off, so she wasn't getting a pass, either.

"I know you want me to beat your ass."

Michelle began to shed tears in hopes I would release the hold I had on her, but she was sadly mistaken.

"Bitch, fuck your tears. You wasn't crying when you was talking that shit." I snatched her head back and squeezed her jaw. "Now, try me again, and I'll break your face. I'll have you in this bitch eating from a straw." Finally letting her go, I pushed her away from me, and that was all it took for her to keep quiet. "Now, go fix me a drink." I was happy my kids were at school so they didn't have to witness their daddy kicking their mother's ass for disrespecting me.

Michelle walked away without a sound. There were so many thoughts running through my head, and the only thing that could help were my meds, but I didn't want to take them.

After two hours of drinking back-to-back, I was wasted, horny, and filled with mixed emotions. The questions in my head overpowered the alcohol and floated around in my brain like alphabet soup. *Was she really pregnant with my baby? Did Giovanni ruin my chances of being with Barbee?* My thoughts were all over the place, and I couldn't focus.

"Michelle." There was no response, so I called out for her several more times. The liquor had me so drunk I couldn't pull myself from the bed and look for her, so I decided to call her phone.

"What?" she snapped, obviously upset with me.

"Where the fuck are you?"

"Outside."

"With who?"

"Nobody."

"Bring your ass in here."

"For what?"

"Because I said so." Taking a deep breath, I paused for a second. "Please, don't make me come out there."

"I'm coming." Her tone had a sudden change in it.

Michelle slammed the door loud enough for me to hear and acknowledge the fact she was upset, but I didn't care. She could slam every door in this bitch. I still wasn't apologizing.

If anything, she should have been apologizing to me for making me act out. We had been together long enough for her to know not to push my buttons. She was also aware of my condition, but apparently she wasn't using that thing in her head called a brain. Well, she learned today.

"What do you want, Richard?" Michelle only called me that when I did something wrong.

She sat on the bed next to me, and I rolled over and wrapped my arms around her belly. "How is my baby doing?"

"Oh, you're worried now? Because earlier you didn't care about me or the baby."

My speech was slurred. "You made me do that to you." I tried pulling her close to me so she could lie down. "Come on."

"I'm not sleepy."

"I didn't ask you that, now lay down."

She complied with my demand. Then I wrapped my body around hers and rubbed her stomach. In the next two months we would be welcoming our fourth child into the world. Barbee's child would've made five, but thanks to Gio, that wasn't going to happen. The two of them would've been the last of the Gathers' bunch. Everybody else was in middle school. My twin girls were in seventh grade, and my son was in sixth grade. My eyes grew heavy, and the last thing I felt was the constant kick of the baby.

Chapter 8

Corey

The first address we were headed to was the one retrieved from her text messages, located in West Palm Beach. I was certain it belonged to this nigga Rich. When I caught this nigga, I was going to put a few holes in his chest.

"How far does it say on the GPS?" Amon asked.

"45 minutes." I looked over at him. "Can you get us there quicker than that?"

"Hell yeah." Amon pressed down on the gas and we took off like we were on the NASCAR track. My body jerked, and I quickly put on my seatbelt. He thought that shit was funny. "You said get you there."

"Nigga, in one piece. I don't want to die before we get there." I trusted my nigga with my life, but I wasn't trying to fly through the windshield.

"Put on some tunes. I can't stand a silent ride."

"Just drive. I got this."

For the mood I was in, it was only right I put on Yo Gotti *CM9*. This was definitely something we could ride to without skipping a song. We needed more rappers in the game like this. Some of these new cats were killing me on the mic and needed to put that bitch down 'cause they weren't lyrical or 'bout that life, but Gotti spoke that gangsta shit, and I was on that. Boppin' my head, I sat back and relaxed while rapping along.

It go bricks, all white bricks
Cocaine music man, I'm on that same shit
Just put a hunnit fifty on my same wrist
I used to whip-whip-whip-whip-whip with Tip
Fuck around got residue on my Patek
Fucked around, got pulled over, tail light out in the Vette

Ridin' dirty and if they search, I know I'm headed to the feds
Once they a nigga for license and registration, you know I flee it
(I'm outta here)
Nigga talkin' 'bout front 'em something, get outta here

No matter how much I rapped, my mind was still on the love of my life. I would never forgive myself if anything happened to her. It was bad enough I wasn't there when she was shot. Now the shit was happening again. I couldn't believe this, but mark my words, this would never happen again. From now on she was going to have a personal bodyguard. She probably wouldn't go for it, but my mind was made up, and there was nothing she could do about it. My job was to protect, and I felt as if I failed not once, but twice now.

"Hey, check the bag and see what he gave us."

I reached into the backseat and sat the bag in my lap. Pulling the contents out, I laughed. "Where the fuck this nigga get this shit from?" I help up a black shirt with white letters that said FBI, along with two badges.

Amon looked over and laughed, too. "Man, that nigga crazy as hell. But that's not a bad idea, though. We can slide easier with that shit."

"Hell yeah."

The ride there was a quick one. Urgency was necessary. Amon parked the car and we changed our shirts before getting out. I passed him his badge, slid mine into my back pocket, and tucked my heat inside my waist band. Carefully scanning the parking lot, I made sure there was no one being nosey.

The address was plastered into my photographic memory, so there was no need to check it again. We stood in front of the condo door, and I knocked with authority. What was good about this situation was he didn't know who we were or the real reason we were there.

There was no answer, so I knocked once more.

"I'm about to peek inside the window. Give me a second." He walked away, and I continued to knock. Amon returned fairly quickly. "I don't see anybody on the inside."

"We going in."

Reaching into my pocket, I pulled out old faithful, my lock picking tools. I was able to gain access within seconds.

My gun was in my hand as I placed one foot over the threshold, making my way inside. Amon was behind me with his strap out. We walked through the apartment quietly, just in case anyone was home. There were two bedrooms, but they both were empty. I stood in the master bedroom, and thoughts of Barbee lying on this mattress made me see red. This was probably where she was that day I couldn't get her on the phone.

"What you looking at?" Amon asked as he made his way to the bathroom.

"Nothing. Just thinking about where she could be. This bed is untouched."

"We gon' find her, bruh. I promise."

"I hope so." I sat down on the bed with my head in my hands. "I feel like this is my fault."

"Why you feel like that?"

"She was supposed to go with me yesterday to take Sierra to the DMV, but I let her stay home."

"That's not your fault. You had no way of knowing this was gon' happen."

"I wasn't there for her once again, and it shouldn't have gone down like this."

"Come on, bruh, I need you focused. We can't find her if your mind ain't there. Let's go check out this other address."

There was nothing anyone could say to make me feel better about what was going on. My biggest fear was she was dead. It had been twenty-four hours, and the chances of finding her were getting slimmer by the minute.

We left the apartment unnoticed and made our way to the next address, which was only twenty minutes away. The GPS led us to a yellow and white house, and someone was home, because there was an SUV parked in the driveway. The grass was trimmed neatly, and so were the bushes. The basketball hoop threw me off because this had to be a family home. *Why would anyone hold her hostage here?* I hoped this search was about to come to an end. If blood had to be shed, then that's what it was gon' be.

We parked directly behind the SUV and approached the front door, ringing the doorbell.

"Be right there." The voice was pleasant and belonged to a woman. When the door opened, Amon and I looked at each other in utter shock. Standing in front of us was a pregnant woman, holding her bulging belly. "Hello," she smiled. "How can I help you?"

Quickly pulling my badge from my back pocket and showing it to her, I introduced myself. "I'm Special Agent Stanley Burress, and this is my partner, Darryl Myers." Amon showed his credentials as well.

She appeared confused. "Oh, well, what can I do for you fellas?"

"We're looking for a Michelle Gathers." I slid my credentials back into my pocket.

"Well, I'm Michelle. Why are you looking for me?" she asked.

"We're investigating the disappearance of Barbee Kingston, and we would like to ask you a few questions." The way she looked at me made me a little suspicious. "Can we come in, please?"

"Um. Yeah. Sure, but I don't think I will be of any help." She stumbled over her words and backed up so we could come in. We walked into the home, and she escorted us into the living room.

My eyes roamed the room. Hanging on the walls and in the china cabinet were family photos with them and their children. From the outside looking in, they seemed like the perfect family, but that was far from the truth. What we were about to show her was about to ruin all of that. "Are you here alone?"

"Yes. My husband just left about a half an hour ago." She sat down on the loveseat.

"Do you know where he went?" I probed a little.

"No." She sat intertwining her fingers.

"Are you okay, ma'am?" Amon asked. "You seem a bit nervous."

"No, I'm just wondering what's going on, that's all."

Leaning forward on the couch, I looked her in the eyes. "We have phone records indicating you spoke with the victim before she went missing."

"I don't know anyone by that name."

Amon passed her a copy of the text messages. "Look familiar?"

Michelle's eyes scanned the paper, and they suddenly became glassy. "This is not my phone number," she admitted.

"Whose number is it?" I needed answers.

"My husband's."

"What's your husband's name?"

"Richard Gathers."

When she said his name, I almost pulled my gun out and told her to get him here pronto. I pictured myself filling his chest with bullet holes. Remembering the conversation I had with Amon earlier, I knew I had to be cool about it if I wanted to find her.

"When are you expecting him home?"

"I'm not sure." Michelle wiped her eyes, and I felt bad for her. Here she was pregnant with his child, and he was cheating on her. I knew it was hard for her to see those text messages. Hell, it was hard for me to read, so I could definitely feel her pain. However, she was going to be shedding more tears than that when I killed him, and if she knew like I knew, she would save those tears for his funeral.

"I don't have any cards, but when he returns, give us a call so we can speak with him." I wrote the number to my burner phone on a piece of paper and handed it to her. "If you don't feel comfortable letting him know that we were here, feel free to call, and we will show up like we were never here."

"I will." She slipped the number into her pocket.

"Let's go, partner." She was about to get up. "We'll let ourselves out. Take a moment to yourself."

She nodded her head. "Wait!" Michelle added. "Do you have a picture of her?"

"Yes," I replied and pulled out my phone. I scrolled through my gallery and found a solo pic of Barbee and showed Michelle. "That's her."

She stared at the photo for a few seconds. "Okay, thanks."

"Good day."

Once we were outside, Amon looked at me. "You think she gon' do it?"

"I don't know. At first I thought she knew something about it, but when she saw those messages, her demeanor changed." I opened the passenger and climbed in. "Something's not right about this, I will say that."

"Yeah, I peeped the way she was answering the questions and how she was looking. That body language was a muthafucka." Amon backed out of the driveway and pulled off. "We may have to stake out his crib for the next few days and see how he moves. If he does have her, he's hiding her someplace."

"I'm down for laying on this nigga in order to get my baby back, man." I pulled the heat from my waistband and slid it underneath the seat. Afterward, I took off the t-shirt and put it back in the bag, along with the badge.

When we were out of the neighborhood and sitting at a red light, Amon took off his shirt and threw it in the back. "It felt funny wearing that damn shirt. That's the closet I ever wanna get to the FBI," he joked.

"Shit, who you telling."

"So, what's next?" Amon asked.

"Man, I don't know, but I gotta check on my sister." I hit her up on her cell.

"Have you found Barbee yet?" Sierra didn't say hello or nothing, but I knew she was worried. Barbee was that mother figure she didn't have growing up.

I exhaled deeply. "Not yet."

"Corey, what are we gon' do?"

"You are gonna stay in that hotel room and let me handle this."

"Do you think," she paused.

"What?"

"That she's dead."

That comment fucked my head up. "No, don't say that. I'm going to find her, don't you worry. I won't rest until I do. I promise."

"I can't sleep worrying about her, Corey. Every time I close my eyes, I can see her face, and she's begging for help."

I closed my eyes to keep any tears from falling. "I have to go. I'll check on you later."

Talking to Sierra made me feel worse than I already did, so I hung up quickly. That girl was liable to make me have a nervous breakdown.

"What's wrong?" Amon asked.

"Man, she just fucked my head up."

"What she said?"

"She asked me if I thought Barbee was dead." My phone fell to the floor, but I didn't bother to pick it up.

"We not even thinking like that, but to be honest, I don't think he would kill her. Look at the text messages he sent. This man is talking about how he loves her."

"What is that supposed to mean?" Amon was acting like he never saw the ID channel before. "Do you know how many people kill females they supposedly love?"

"Yeah, I see your point."

"Hey, have you talked to Mercedes?"

"Nah, I didn't want to say anything at first because I didn't want the family to be worried. They've suffered enough."

"I think we need to tell them."

"That's the easiest way for us to get caught for killing him. I know my uncle, and he will call the police."

He was right. The love Papa had for his daughter was like none other. "I think we should at least talk to Mercedes."

"Call her and see what she can tell us."

Picking my phone up from the floor, I dialed her number, but it went straight to voicemail. I tried two more times. "Her phone going straight to the voicemail, man."

Amon then reached for his phone. "I'll call the house phone." The phone rang a few times through the speakers before he picked up the phone. "Hey, Papa, what you doing?"

"Sitting on the couch, watching T.V."

"Oh, okay. Is Mercedes home?"

"No, she not here. I haven't seen her in two days."

"She didn't move, did she?"

"No. All her stuff still here, and she never said she was moving."

"Okay. I'll talk to you later."

"Is everything okay?" Papa wasn't hanging up that easily.

"Yeah."

"Alright then."

I waited for him to hang up. "Something ain't right about this shit, dawg. I'm telling you."

"I know what we gotta do, but first I have to go by the house."

***

Rich

Hitting the alarm on my car, I threw the shopping bags over onto the passenger seat. I had just left the Boca mall from picking up a few items for Barbee. What she didn't know was we were going out tonight. I found her a sexy dress and some nice heels to wear. We were going to the strip club in Dade while my cousin babysat Mercedes. I looked into the mirror and laughed at myself because I couldn't believe I was going down this same road again. Just like every other Tom, Dick, and Harry, I have skeletons in my closet, and I don't like to be judged. No sin is greater than the next, and I needed everyone to know that. God took care of fools and babies, and I definitely wasn't a baby. He understood I didn't take rejection too well, and that's when I would have to unleash the beast on these bitches, so they would know I was nothing to play with. That wasn't my first rodeo, and it probably wasn't going to be the last.

It all started with a chick named Tasha. I met her at a sports bar after being married for two years. My wife was pregnant, and I was bored at home with that pregnant sex. Tasha was on the dance floor, dancing seductively with her girls. I waited until she stepped to the bar to order a drink. She was wearing a pair of booty shirts and knee-high strappy heels. Very sexy, to say the least. My dick was hard watching her dance.

"Let me pay for that, beautiful."

"Sure, but you have to pay for my girls, too."

I didn't give a damn about that as long as it was beneficial for me in the end. "Order away."

For the rest of the night, we engaged in some deep conversation. She told me she was a supervisor at a call center, and she had a daughter. By the end of the night, I had her and her girls fucked up. We walked through the parking lot, and out of the blue her homegirl's old man was in the parking lot, waiting on her. He cursed her out and forced her into the car. "Tasha, you need to find a way home, because I told her not to go out."

So, of course, I offered her a ride, but I didn't take her home. We ended up at a hotel. I beat the brakes off her ass until morning. "I feel so embarrassed. I don't normally do stuff like this." She covered her face. "I had too much to drink."

"You have no reason to. I still have respect for you. Shit, we grown."

Five months later, she called the shit off. "Rich, my baby daddy came home, and we're going to work things out."

"Bitch, are you crazy? I've helped you with your daughter while that nigga was serving a petty-ass bid. You got me fucked up."

"Please, don't call me anymore. It's over." That bitch had the nerve to hang up on me.

But no. No, she was crazy if she thought I was gon' let that shit slide after I helped take care of her daughter. She stopped *taking my calls and all. One day I caught her in the same sports bar, but I played it cool.*

"What's up, Tasha?" I whispered in her ear while she sat at the bar. She turned around in her seat and her eyes lit up. "Calm down, baby, ain't no love lost. It's all good. Let me buy you a drink for old times."

"Okay."

When she wasn't looking, I slipped a little something in her drink and took her back to the bunny ranch. Tasha was out cold, but that didn't stop me from getting what I wanted. The next morning she woke up next to me with a sticky pussy, so she knew what time it was.

"How did I get here?" She rubbed her head. I knew headaches were an after effect of the date rape drug.

"You left the bar with me last night," I chuckled. "I guess you had too much to drink."

"No, I didn't. I wasn't drunk."

"I guess that means you wanted to leave with me."

Tasha got up and grabbed her clothes and dressed herself quickly. "Take me home, now," she demanded.

"Who you talking to like that?"

"You!" she yelled. "Now, take me home. Now! I don't want anything to do with you."

I stepped to her. "Say that again."

"Get the fuck out my face and take me home before I call the police and tell them you kidnapped me."

"I didn't force you to come here."

"Okay." She pulled her phone from her purse and dialed the number, but I slapped it out of her hand.

"Bitch, I wish you would call the police on me."

She picked the phone up and ran out of the room. I chased her and pushed her to the floor. Climbing on top of her, I slapped her a few times, but she fought back. Tasha was no match for me. I pinned her to the floor.

"Rich, stop," she begged.

"Not until you take me back."

"I don't want to be with you. Just leave me alone." Her phone rang, and the ringtone was a song by Mary J. Blige.

"That's yo' baby daddy calling you."

"Yes. Now, let me go."

"You love that nigga?" I tested her, but she didn't answer me. "Answer my question before I hurt you."

"Rich, just stop, please."

"Do you love me?"

When she shook her head no, I lost it. The next thing I knew, my hands were around her neck and I was choking her. Tasha clawed at my hands, but I wouldn't let go of her throat. I squeezed and squeezed until her legs stopped moving. After realizing she was dead, I stopped.

Later on that evening, I waited until the coast was clear to move her body out of there. I dumped her body behind a dumpster a few blocks away from the sports bar and went home. A few days later, the police came to question me, but I had an airtight alibi thanks to my wife.

Barbee was going to love the gifts I bought her. I just hoped she was going to be on her best behavior, because shit could get real bad for her. I was still pissed at her for that stunt she pulled, but I was giving her the opportunity to redeem herself and work on gaining my trust once again. I couldn't wait to see her face when I got there. I knew it would be priceless, especially when she found out what I had planned for us.

Chapter 9

Corey

Amon and I sat in the car, stalking our prey until he graced us with his presence. We were back in uniform, but I was sure he would know we weren't agents. I was certain he was smarter than that. In my lap sat a 24-carat solid gold desert eagle with a black grip handle. This special occasion caused me to pull out my favorite piece of artillery. A man of his status was sure to have some heavy shit in it, but my plan was to ambush him and obtain the upper hand. Calculated steps were necessary for this attack that was about to unravel. One hour passed easily, and I wasn't watching the clock. It didn't matter what time he got there. I wasn't moving until he did.

"He need to hurry up."

"I agree, but we not moving until he gets here."

"I know that." He held up his pistol. "We putting an end to this shit today. Somebody gon' feel my pain today."

"Who you telling. I'm ready to bust a nigga head open like a watermelon." When I looked up, I could see a limo approaching us. "Get ready. I think this the nigga, right here."

I finger fucked the trigger and pulled the hammer back. "As soon as they get to the gate, make a run for it."

"Got it."

The limo continued to make its way up the street, doing the speed limit. The driver hit the signal, and I knew it was him. Once he hooked the right, we got out and bum-rushed that shit. Amon put his gun on the temple of the driver.

"Unlock the doors."

I was standing in the back, waiting to hear the click from the doors. Pulling open the door handle, I observed the man in the back.

"What are you doing?" Giovanni asked.

"Shut the fuck up and scoot over. Don't ask me any questions." My voice was filled with rage, so he did exactly what I told him.

Amon got in the passenger seat next to the driver. "Go."

"If it's money you want," he started, but I aimed my gun at him.

"Didn't I say 'shut the fuck up?'" He nodded his head. "You'll find out what I want soon enough."

"Where are your bodyguards?" Amon asked.

"They're not here, and something tells me you're not really agents."

Amon looked back to where we were sitting. "You mean to tell me a man of your caliber doesn't have 24-hour protection?"

Giovanni cleared his throat. "Forgive me, but no one is stupid enough to rob me. Everyone who knows me is aware of what I can do. But something tells me you don't know me at all." He remained calm.

"Watch your mouth, old man," I warned him by tapping his temple with the barrel of the gun. "Who's in the house?"

"My maid."

"I'm warning you that if you try anything, I will smoke yo' ass." The limo came to a stop. "Let's go."

Giovanni did what he was told. The driver looked terrified. "Everything will be ok, John. I'm sure all of this is just one big misunderstanding."

I nudged him in the back. "Yeah, we'll see about that."

I watched him closely as he unlocked the door and pushed him through when it was ajar. Amon was behind me, making sure the driver didn't try anything.

On the inside, I patted them both down. "You're not armed, are you?"

"If I was, you would've been shot a long time ago."

Sarcasm was not what I wanted to hear, so to let him know I wasn't playing with him, I hit him across the head.

"Ugh." He groaned, holding his head in the same spot I hit him.

"Keep that up and it's gonna be worse than that, old man. Both of you take a seat," I instructed them, waving the gun in the direction I wanted them to go.

"Call for the maid."

He picked up a walkie-talkie from the table. "Consuela, come down here, please." He sat the device back down on the table. "You still haven't told me what this is about, 'cause I have a gut feeling you're portraying yourself to be something you're not."

"Well, follow your gut. It may lead you right." Reaching into my pocket, I pulled out my cellphone and revealed a picture of Barbee. His eyes stretched like flying saucers. "Judging by your facial expression, something tells me you know why I'm here now?"

"I don't know."

"Don't lie to me, and I'm not playing games with you. I'll smoke yo' ass so quick you wouldn't know what hit you." I stepped a little closer to him. "So, you telling me you don't know her?"

"I saw her before, that's it."

"Nah, you know more than that." Leaning forward, I pressed that warm lead to his thigh, because if he didn't tell me what I needed to know, I was pulling the trigger. "Now, start talking."

Amon was standing close by, keeping an eye on John. My concentration was broken when I heard someone coming down the stairs. I pictured the maid to be someone older, but to my surprise, she was a young chick.

"Oh my God!" she screeched, covering her mouth. "What's going on?"

"Get over here and have a seat, cutie." Amon smiled, then looked at Giovanni. "This a sexy maid you got. You sure all she does is clean your house?" He laughed while licking his lips. "I gotta get myself one of these."

Giovanni didn't find it funny, not one bit.

Turning my attention back to the man in front of me, I pressed down harder on his thigh. "You were saying?"

Giovanni exhaled loudly, demonstrating his frustration. "She came here with one of my workers she was dating. I don't know her too well because we only saw each other twice."

Pow!

I shot him in the thigh.

"Argh!" Giovanni screamed, and so did the maid. "I told you what you wanted to know."

"No, you didn't. You're missing out on a lot of details, and I'll keep shooting you in every one of your limbs until you bleed out and die."

Giovanni's breathing was heavy. "Okay, okay. I knew her sister, Nehiya. Barbee hooked us up. We got together here and there, but that's it. I don't really know them like that."

Pow!

The bullet pierced his other thigh, and he squealed like a pig. "I swear, that's all that happened. I never saw them again."

One thing I despised was a liar, and he was insulting my intelligence. Therefore, I needed to hit him where it hurt to make him admit to killing Chyna and my unborn child, and almost killing the woman I love. The way he looked at the maid when she came down told me she was more than that. She was my new bullseye for target practice, so I aimed and shot her in the shoulder.

"Ah!" she screamed, holding on to her wound.

"She has nothing to do with this! Leave her alone," Giovanni begged. "Do what you want with me, just leave her alone, please."

Amon looked over at Giovanni while he had his strap aimed at her head. "Tell us what we wanna know, or I'ma kill her. I don't give a fuck about her, just like you didn't give a fuck about my cousins."

"What?" he muttered.

"Don't play dumb, nigga. You sent your little henchmen to kill my family."

Giovanni finally gave in and dropped the dime on the execution of Nehiya, how she snitched, and how he wanted to seek revenge on Barbee. I sat there biting my lip and trying to keep my trigger finger under control. I needed every piece of info he had to offer.

"And what about your boy? The one Barbee was dating?" I asked.

"Rich?"

"Yeah, him."

"What about him?"

"Did you send him to kidnap Barbee?" I asked.

"No."

His response was too quick, and that didn't sit too well with me. "Call him right now," I demanded. "See if he has her, and find out where he is." Giovanni reached for the phone in his pocket. I pointed the gun at his hand. "Slowly, and put it on speaker."

The phone rang a few times before Rich finally picked up. "Whadup, G?"

"Did you find her yet?"

"Nah. That bitch hid herself pretty good. I went by the address you gave me, but no one lives there anymore. There's a 'For Sale' sign out front."

111

My blood pressure went high as the sky. As bad as I wanted to snatch the phone, I knew I couldn't or we'd never find her or she'd be dead. Giovanni wasn't as good as he thought he was, because he didn't detect the lie that was just told to him. I knew he had Barbee, and he was about to disclose his location.

"What's your twenty?"

"Bunny Ranch."

"Doing?"

"Getting ready for when I do find her."

"Keep me posted. I gotta go."

As soon as he hung up, I was on his trail. "What the fuck is the Bunny Ranch?"

"That's what he calls his condo."

"Where is it?"

"Give me a piece of paper and I'll write it down." He scribbled an address on a piece of paper and handed it to me. "That's where he lives."

The address he provided was the same address that we already had, but I acted as if I didn't know it before handing it over to Amon. "This better be the right address."

"I swear it is." He looked over at his maid. "Consuela, are you okay?"

"I don't know."

"Can you leave now? I've cooperated with you, and she needs to go to the hospital," he pleaded.

Laughing hysterically, I looked at Amon. "Man, you hear this nigga?"

"Yeah, I heard him, but I think he's delusional. Maybe he lost too much blood or some shit," Amon chuckled.

"Had to if he think this bitch gon' make it to the hospital."

John, the driver, had been quiet the whole time. I guess he thought that would be his ticket to live.

"Please, don't kill me. I didn't see anything," she cried.

"Yeah, that's what they all say until the police question them and issue out some empty threats. Then suddenly your memory comes back," Amon added.

"No, I promise, I won't tell a soul."

"Sorry, cutie, I have to let you go." Amon fired a single shot into Consuela's chest.

"No!" The sound of Giovanni's voice echoed through the house following the gunshot. "You didn't have to kill her," he cried.

"You didn't have to kill Nehiya or Chyna, but you did," Amon spat before firing a shot through John's forehead.

I knelt down in front of Giovanni. "Look at me. Do you see the pain you caused me by shooting Barbee and killing our baby?" It hurt my heart to bring that subject up, but it was necessary. "I want my face to be the last one you see before you die."

"Your eyes say you're not a killer."

Rising to my feet with tears in my eyes, I aimed my gun at him for the last time. "It's what's behind the eyes that counts."

I closed my eyes and fired three shots into his chest.

***

Barbee

It had been two days, and we were still stuck in the damn basement. This made me wonder if anyone had put out a missing person's report, because someone should've found us by then. I guess it wasn't the First 48. It was difficult as fuck to sleep sitting up. My damn neck had a crook in it, and my body felt stiff as fuck. Our babysitter was knocked out on the futon, calling the hogs.

"I'm sorry, Mercedes. It's my fault you are in this mess."

"No, I should've known better than to believe anything out his mouth."

I was confused because I never asked how she ended up here in the first place. "What did he tell you?"

"He told me you were at his place, and you were depressed about what was going on. I never stopped to think he could be lying. I guess I was just thrown off because I had been drinking."

"Where were you?"

"At the strip club you met him at. I told him I would follow him, but he insisted I rode with him. That's why I was surprised to see you tied up to a chair when I got here."

"Rich is crazy." I looked up to make sure his friend was still asleep.

"No shit."

"No, I mean certified, pink slip crazy. I found some prescriptions in the bathroom, and he has borderline personality disorder."

Mercedes' eyebrows rose a notch. "You mean to tell me we're being held captive by a fucking psychopath?"

"Unfortunately."

"Just when I thought my life couldn't get any worse."

"Tell me about it."

"I have to pee."

"Oh, shit."

Just as I was about to call out to the babysitter, I heard the door open. Rich walked in carrying some shopping bags. This crazy bitch was smiling like there was nothing wrong with this picture. He walked over and kissed me on the cheek.

"Did you miss me, boo?"

My mind was telling me to say *I missed you like I miss having a rash on my ass,* but I decided not to add fuel to the fire I was already in. The babysitter's snoring kicked up a notch, and he turned around quickly. "Aye, yo," he called out, but his boy didn't move, so he walked over and woke him up. "Now you sleeping on the job?"

"Shit, where they going?"

Rich walked away and came back to where we were sitting. "Now, where was I?" He looked up at the ceiling. "Oh yeah, did you miss me?"

"Yes," I lied. "My sister has to pee, so can you please let her get up?"

"What do I get for doing you a favor?"

"Can you please let her go to the bathroom?"

"First, you gotta tell me." He thought this shit was a game, but once I got free, I was gon' kill this bastard.

"I'll do whatever you want." At this point I didn't have a choice. As long as she didn't have to sit in piss, I was fine with it. I guess that was my guilt weighing me down.

"Okay, pretty number two, I'll take you to the bathroom." He sat the bags on the floor and untied her from the chair. "Don't move yet." He placed his hand underneath the seat where the bomb was located. I was trying to see what he was doing without making it obvious, but I couldn't see anything. "Okay, now get up." Rich smiled at me. "I have something for you when I come back."

"Okay," I replied. There was no telling what he had, but I was about to find out as soon as he got back from chaperoning my sister.

They were gone for approximately ten minutes before they re-entered the basement. Mercedes' mood appeared to be different. She had a vacant stare on her face. When she sat down, I looked her up and down, and then at Rich.

"What did you do to her?"

He had the audacity to smirk. "Nothing. She needed some extra time in the bathroom. Is that okay with you?"

Ignoring him, I turned my attention back to Mercedes. "Did he do something to you?"

"No. I don't feel well."

There was definitely something wrong. I wasn't buying that lie, but there was nothing I could do or say until he was out of the basement.

"Okay."

"Now that we got our concerns out of the way, we can move onto something more important." He looked back at the babysitter. "Are you listening?"

"Yeah," he responded.

"Good." Rich turned around and mugged me with this wolfish look. "Since you took something from me, you gon' work tonight in order to pay me back."

"Pay you back for what?"

"The work y'all stole from Giovanni. Do you know that brought on a drought for me? I couldn't get any work because of that little stunt you orchestrated. That meant I couldn't make any money."

"And how do you think I'm supposed to pay you back for that?" This man had a fucking problem. Sounds like he was about to try and extort money from me.

"The same way you make money. You about to set up a few dudes for me."

"What?" His response caught me off guard.

"You heard me. We're going out tonight, and you're going to show me how you run your little operation, and make me some money in the process."

Now I was aggravated, but somehow I knew he meant what he said. "You can't be serious?"

"As a heart attack, baby." He stood up and untied me. "Now, let's go and get dressed. I'm sure you're going to love the dress and shoes I bought you." He turned to his cousin.

"Bruh, keep ya eyes on her, and if you don't hear from me by midnight, kill her."

"Fo' sho," He responded.

Upstairs in the bedroom, he showed me what he purchased, and to my surprise it was gorgeous and just the right size. My shoes came from Aldi, and I fell in love with them.

"Who picked this out for you, and how did you know my size?"

"I study the things I love. Do you like it?"

"Yeah, I do."

Beating Rich at his game was the only thing on my mind, and I had to make sure I was playing it well. He had gone to great lengths to get me here, but contrary to my fears, I didn't believe he wanted to really kill me.

A shower was what I needed and I was astonished when he didn't try to join me. Turning the nob, cold water gushed out, so I waited until it warmed up before I stepped in. The ceramic tile chilled my feet. I stood underneath the chrome shower-head, and it felt like cold raindrops covering my frame. The chill bumps on my arm disappeared as I adjusted to the temperature, making me warm. Closing my eyes, I splashed water on my face.

It was funny how people take for granted the small things until they're no longer at their disposal. Taking a shower was the highlight of my day, but I'm sure my night was about to get a little more interesting.

Using the washcloth given to me, I lathered it up with soap and scrubbed my body. After covering every inch with suds, I rinsed myself off and repeated those steps once more. Upon completion, I felt like a new woman. The last time I touched water was when I gave myself a wipe-off after having sex with my captor.

Stepping from the shower, my feet were greeted by a soft rug. I dried off and walked to the room to get dressed. Rich was waiting on me patiently, fully clothed.

I smiled. "I see you trust me now."

"Just for the moment. You still have a lot to prove to me."

"I'm not going to run." I let the towel I was wrapped in fall to floor, and his eyes stretched. "I'm going to wait until you free me."

Rich was completely mesmerized by my chocolate frame. He didn't blink once. "And what if I don't free you?"

"You plan on keeping me here as a hostage?" My hands were on my hips, and my head was tilted.

"If you come to your senses, you could be my wife. Then you'll be here by choice and not force."

"Well, it depends on what you're willing to do for me."

"And what does that mean?"

"You'll find out soon enough."

Rich broke his stare. "I'm not playing games with you."

"Oh, I'm not playing any games with you, either."

He looked at his watch. "Get dressed so we can go."

It only took twenty minutes to get ready since I didn't have any makeup. That made me feel naked. I stood in the mirror. Well, at least my eyebrows and lashes were on point.

"Are you ready yet?"

"Yeah, since I don't have any makeup."

"You don't need makeup. You look good without it. I don't know why you wear that foolishness, anyway."

I cut my eyes at him. "Yeah, okay, 'cause last time I checked, I had on makeup when we met."

"Learn to be natural is all I'm saying. Just because your name Barbee doesn't mean you have to look like one."

"Whatever." His humor was not amusing to me at all.

We ended up at a strip club in Miami called The Office. Rich set me up at a table and made sure he didn't sit too close to me, but not far enough I couldn't hear his instructions. The waitress delivered me a bottle of Patron, and I fixed myself a cup. I had no intention of drinking, but I guess I had to make it believable.

"So, who am I looking for?" I asked.

He slid me his phone. "Him."

It was some dude on Instagram that went by the name The Real Paper Chaser. I took a good look at his picture and scrolled through a few more to get an idea of why we were robbing him, but it was clear when I stumbled upon him flashing money in a hotel room. That was one thing no one could make me understand: posting money pics. They might as well make a post saying they were looking for a jack boy to take that money off their hands. Hungry and envious niggas were always looking for a quick come-up. I guess moving in silence was too much to ask for. Nowadays it was cool to upload a person's life on social media to make people think they had more than they actually did. Stupidity at its finest. I was taught to keep muthafuckas out of my game room so they wouldn't know my next move.

I slid the phone back to Rich and picked up my drink.

The vibe was nice, and some of the chicks were bad, but there were far too many fake asses for me. The problem wasn't the fact of them going under the knife, but they weren't done tastefully. Some of the asses were too big for the owner's body, and their legs were too skinny. My advice to them was make sure the booty fits, and I hated to see a deflated ass, or one cheek that was bigger than the other.

Checking out the crowd, I spotted my target for the night. He was surrounded by a gang of dudes, and they were wildin' out. My target was definitely young. The way he carried on let me know he was new to the game, and he wasn't used to having money. This type could be very easy, or he could be difficult. It depended on the individual and how arrogant he was, but I was a pro, and I was pulling this off tonight.

While I observed him for the next thirty minutes, I paid attention to the women who caught his eye, and I knew I fit the category. The only problem was I wasn't wearing any makeup. There was something about that facial that attracted certain breeds. I sipped my drink, and that's when it hit me.

"Rich, give me $50."

He moved his cup from his lips. "For what?"

"Do you want to get him or not?" I asked. One thing I wasn't about to do was get into an argument with this nut. "I'm a professional, and I know what I'm doing, trust me." He pulled his money from his pocket, and he was racked up, shawty. "As a matter of fact, give me $150."

Surprisingly, he handed the money over with no further questions. "I'll be right back."

The look in his eyes told me he really didn't trust me. "You know the deal."

"I'm not doing anything funny, I promise. And besides, we're too far away to try and pull a stupid stunt."

"We'll see."

Strutting away from him, I was searching for the dressing room when I bumped into an old associate of mine. "Barbee, is that you?" she smiled.

"In the flesh," I smiled back. We gave each other a hug.

"I heard about your sisters, and I'm sorry for your loss."

Bad news sure did travel fast in Lauderdale. One thing about my hood was they shouted the bad from the mountaintops, but they whispered about success.

"Thanks, I appreciate that."

"Girl, what have you been up to?"

"I'm getting ready to open up my own strip club."

Her eyes lit up with happiness. "That's good. I'm so proud of you." Star spun around in a full circle. "I'm looking for work, if you hiring."

I had to admit, Star looked damn good in her two piece, rocking her coke bottle shape with her flawless mocha skin. "You'll be a perfect fit."

"Good. Take my number, 'cause I don't have my phone."

"I left my phone at home, so I'll have to give you mine," I explained. "Follow me to the dressing room."

She was filled with glee.

"Hey, do y'all have someone here that does makeup?"

"Yeah, she's back here now. Why, you need an artist for your club?"

"Maybe, but I need her right now."

"Oh, okay. I'll introduce you to her."

Chapter 10

Barbee

Half an hour later, I walked out of the dressing room slayed. My face was so flawless I had to take her card. I would definitely be doing business with her at my club. Rich was getting a lap dance when I returned. He looked at me and winked.

"You want a dance?"

"I'm straight. I'll leave that to you." I fixed myself a drink. Normally I wouldn't indulge in alcohol while working, but since I was working with Rich, I felt comfortable doing so. It was different with a man. When it was just us females, I couldn't afford to do so. By nature, men were stronger, so I had to keep a level head at all times. Besides, I knew he wouldn't let another man harm me.

Rich paid the stripper, then sent her on her way. "You know, I wasn't trying to insinuate that you liked females. I just thought it would be nice to see you get a dance from one."

"That turns you on, huh?"

"Hell yeah. What man wouldn't want to see that? Besides your hair dresser." Rich laughed, then took a sip of his drink.

"My hairdresser is a female."

"I'm sure he is."

Looking across the room, I saw my target was finally standing alone. I stood up and fixed my dress so I could walk over there. "Anyway, I have to go."

"Where are you going?"

"It's that time."

Rich caught on quickly. "Do ya thang."

On the way over, I saw Star talking to him, so I paused for a second. There was no way I would be able to get his attention while he was talking to a half-naked female, so I stood next to the bar until she walked away. Star was headed in my direction, so I stopped her.

"Who is the guy you was just talking to?"

"Who?" she asked.

"The guy with the Louis Vuitton hat on."

"Oh," she laughed. "That's Zay."

"You know him?"

"Yeah." She grinned. "Do you like him?"

"I don't know him, but I need you to do something for me."

"Okay."

When I walked past Zay, his eyes followed me, but he didn't say anything. That was a plus, because now I had his attention. He was on the side of the stage, so I stood a few feet away from him. My drink was in my left hand while I bopped a little to Rick Ross' *I Think She Like Me*, which happened to be my favorite song. From my peripheral vision I could see him smiling at me, but I acted as if I didn't see him.

As soon as I turned back around to face the stage, someone bumped into me, spilling my drink on my dress. "What the fuck?" I shouted. "You just ruined my dress."

"I'm sorry," Star replied. "I'll get you some paper towels."

Zay heard the commotion and walked over. "Everything straight, Star?"

"Yeah, I spilled her drink by accident. I'll be right back."

He looked at me. "You okay, li'l mama?"

"Besides my ruined dress?" I pouted. "I guess I'm okay."

"Don't be mad, that's my homegirl. How about I get you another drink?"

Smiling, I responded, "Thanks."

Star walked up with some napkins. "Here you go, and again, I'm sorry."

"It's okay, Star. Can you bring her another drink?" He grabbed the napkins from her hand. "Tell her what you drinking."

"Patron and lime juice with light ice."

"Be right back." Star winked at me and walked away, smiling.

Zay took it upon himself to clean my dress. We locked eyes and he smiled wide, exposing his platinum grill. He looked better up close. His eyes were light brown, and his complexion was a pecan tan, and his skin was covered in tattoos, all the way down to his hands.

"Thanks."

"I gotchu, no worries."

Star walked up and interrupted our little moment. "Here's your drink."

"Thanks."

For the next hour and a half we vibed hard and had a good time. His squad was cool as fuck. They knew how to make a girl feel welcome, like I was a part of the crew. Zay and I laughed, danced, and threw money on the strippers. From the other side of the room I could feel Rich throwing daggers at me. Ask me if I cared? Nope. This was the most fun I'd had in a while now. He was so down to earth I damn near pulled the plug on Rich's plan. Yeah, the dude was flashy, but he didn't deserve it. He was only 21 and trying to enjoy life, which was understandable. Laughing at my thoughts made me giggle. I had to admit I sounded real soft right now, considering this was my hustle months ago.

Zay looked me. "You enjoyed yourself?"

That was past tense, I thought to myself. "I did."

"Me and my dudes about to hit it."

"Why so soon?" The disappointment in my voice was like a thick lump in my throat, and I was sure he peeped that.

"They ready to call it a night."

"Okay. Thanks for the drinks and the dances."

"You're welcome."

Zay hugged me and walked away, so I made my way back to the other side of the room. Pushing my way through the crowd, I felt someone grab my arm. I was definitely not in the mood to be aggravated because I knew Rich was about to mad the plan failed.

"Stop grabbing me!" I shouted while turning around with an attitude, ready to snap on whomever the harasser was.

Zay laughed. "Look at you, ready to snap on somebody. I was wondering if you wanted to slide with me."

I'm sure the cheesy smile made me look goofy. "Where we sliding to?" Playing dumb wasn't my forte, but it was appropriate at the moment.

"Nowhere in particular."

Not wanting to sound too eager, I pretended to be nervous about leaving with him. "Umm, I don't know if that's a good idea, being that I just met you."

"You don't have nothing to worry about. I promise, you safe with me."

"You promise?" I repeated.

"I gotchu."

"Okay."

"Where's your car?" he asked.

Shit, that completely threw me off, but I had to think fast. "I didn't drive."

"How did you get here?"

"My cousin, but we good. I'll let her know I left."

"A'ight."

When I glanced to my right, Rich was standing in the corner, watching my every move. Zay grabbed my hand and escorted me outside until we were standing beside a Benz truck.

"This your truck?" I asked.

"Nah, we about to rob whoever drives it."

My eyebrows lowered a tad bit. "Huh?" Maybe he wasn't what I thought he was, and maybe Rich was setting me up after all.

Suddenly his seriousness turned into laughter. "I'm joking, but you should've seen your face when I said that."

I slapped him playfully on his arm. "I'm not playing with you."

"You like it, tho?"

"Yeah. I thought about getting this, but I went with the new Lexus instead."

"Look at you." Zay unlocked the door and helped me get inside, before closing my door. That Patron had me lit, so I leaned back in the seat, propping my head on the headrest. The driver's door finally opened, and he climbed in and fixed himself another drink before we pulled off.

We slid around other clubs in Dade for the next forty minutes before we finally stopped at a gas station. Rich had been following us since we left the club, and observing the scowl on his face, I knew he was livid when he approached the passenger window.

"What the fuck taking y'all so long?"

"He wanted to ride around for a little bit." Glancing toward the door, I had to make sure Zay wasn't coming out. "Get back in the car before you make him suspicious."

"Look inside your purse, the zipper part, and put one of those pills in the nigga's drink."

"What is it?"

"Just do it."

"Okay, bye." Then I rolled up the window in his face, but he didn't move. "What now, Rich?" The nastiest frown was on my face.

"That pill will knock him out cold, so as soon as he is, take everything and meet me outside the hotel. I'll be parked by his truck."

Nutso walked away in the nick of time, because Zay was walking out the door. I slipped the pill into his drink, praying it dissolved instantly.

We were back on the road again and he was taking back-to-back sips while we conversed in between songs. Twenty minutes later, his movements were slow and his speech was slurred.

"Are you okay?" I was concerned because I didn't want him to wreck out.

"My head spinning like a muthafucka."

"You probably should lay down. You did have a lot to drink."

"Yeah, you right."

We made it to the hotel – Comfort Suites, to be exact – and he parked in the back. "Why did you park back here?"

"I'm on the first floor," he slurred. "We can go in through the side door."

"Oh, okay."

"Look in the glove box and get the hotel key."

Zay stumbled to the room, and as soon as he was close to the bed, he dived into it head first, stretching out completely with everything on. "I feel funny as fuck."

"It's the alcohol, baby." My mission was to persuade him into thinking that.

He stretched his arm out. "Come lay with me."

Climbing onto the bed, I kicked my heels off. He wasn't out just yet, but it was coming soon. Zay tried kissing on me, but that drug was weighing him down slowly, but surely. However, his hands did manage to find their way to my ass. Giving it a firm squeeze, he moaned, "Damn, that ass soft."

128

That was the last thing he said to me before he passed out. Quickly jumping from the bed, I scrambled around the room, looking for anything of value. There was nothing in sight, and I was becoming impatient. That's when it hit me: the room has a safe. I checked the drawers, but there was no key in sight. I knew it wasn't far away.

"His pockets," I whispered.

Careful not to startle him, I slid my hand in slowly and pulled out the key. When I unlocked the safe, I wasn't prepared for what I saw. There were stacks of money and pieces, another word for other people's identity. He did fraud. There had to be at least $50K, stashed away. There was a Luis Vuitton backpack on the dresser, so I grabbed it and filled it up. More than likely I wasn't getting a cut, so I only took half and left him with the other half. He had work, so he could get that back easily. I took one last glance at Zay before I slipped away like a thief on the night.

Rich waited until we got back to the house before he looked to see how much money was in there. A smile spread across his lips when he dumped the cash onto the bed.

"Damn, baby, I guess you know what you doing."

"I told you that."

"Yeah, you good." Rubbing his hands together, he cut his eyes at me, but his stare was cold. It made me uncomfortable. Suddenly, his hands stopped moving. "You know I don't like how that nigga was all over you."

"Here we go." I knew this was going to be an issue. He had already proven he was a jealous stalker and would stop at nothing to get what he wanted. The lengths he would go to were endless. "I had a job to do, and I'm trying to keep my buzz, if you don't mind." Maybe antagonizing him wasn't the best idea, but fuck him. I was glad he was mad. Served him right for all this damn chaos he caused in my life.

"It didn't take all that to get the job done."

"I've been doing this long enough to know how to bait my targets. I don't tell you how to cook and sell dope, so don't tell me how to do my job, thank you."

"Whatever! You act like you wanted to fuck the nigga."

This fool was real deal talking like we were a couple and I had just betrayed him. This was his idea, and I needed him to keep that in mind. I was doing just fine without his crazy-ass in my life.

"Look, you wanted me to bait him and lure him out of the club, and that's exactly what I did. I can't help that the way I operate makes you feel some type of way."

Rich eyeballed me for a few seconds. "What y'all did in the truck?"

The man was dead-ass serious. All I could do was shake my head at his stupidity. "Are you serious right now? How could we have done anything in the truck with him driving and you tailing us?"

All of a sudden he was quiet, like he was thinking about what I said. When his mouth moved, I knew that shit was short-lived. "Did y'all fuck in the hotel room?"

Now I was ready to slap the shit out of him because he was trying to kill my heavy buzz. "Do you know how stupid you sound right now? I wasn't in there long enough to fuck him, 'cause if I did, we would still be there fucking right now."

"Barbee, don't fucking play with me, and if you didn't fuck him, let me see."

"No. Leave me alone. Shit."

This was complete bullshit, and my mind was telling me I needed to come up with a plan quick, fast, and in a hurry. "I did what you asked me to do, so let's just drop it and change the subject." If he didn't have a bomb under that damn chair, I would take his gun and shoot his ass. "Can you just let my sister go? I'll stay here with you until you get tired of me."

"Nah, that won't work for me. And besides, I'll never get tired of you."

"Why not?" On the inside I was fighting back the tears that desperately wanted to fall.

"You might try to leave me."

"You got me, just let her go. She has nothing to do with this. This is between me and you. Mercedes didn't hurt you, I did."

"Start doing me right and I'll let her go. You have to prove yourself to me."

The liquor was finally taking over my body, and I became lightheaded. I fell back on the bed and closed my eyes. Rich waited a few minutes before he took it upon himself to remove my heels and pull me to the middle of the bed.

"What are you doing?" I whispered.

"Shh. Just relax."

There was no fight in me, so I just lay there with my eyes closed. I could feel my dress rise, followed by the warmth of his tongue on my clitoris. He did all that talking about me fucking another nigga, but that didn't stop him from devouring my pussy. Unconsciously, I rocked my hips and ground my pelvis against his mouth until my legs started to shake, squirting my juices into his mouth. Lying on top of me, I could feel his head parting my lips, making way for his dick to go in deep, touching the bottom. I gasped for air, taking it all in. The act alone was wrong, but it felt good. Maybe that was the liquor talking. Rich's rapid strokes were like a sewing machine, and he stayed at that same pace until he collapsed on top of my sweaty body.

Destiny Skai

Chapter 11

Sierra

There I was, lying in this queen sized bed at the Marriot, alone and staring at the ceiling. My mind was far off in the clouds, thinking about my baby daddy, Dre – the man who captured my heart, loved me for a little while, and then abandoned me. He would never understand how bad he hurt me. Suicide crossed my mind a few times, but then I found out I was having his baby. I'll admit I was happy about it because I knew it would bring him back into my life, that is until that loneliness kicked in because he wasn't with me.

Regardless of what was going on, Dre should be here with me so we could raise our child together. But no, he just had to marry that bitch Tokee. But that didn't matter because I was determined to get him back, married and all. Dre was divorcing that bitch, just as soon as I got him where I wanted him to be.

My phone was next to me, so I picked it up and scrolled through my gallery. There were so many photos of us when we were happy, or so I thought. Dre was everything I wanted in a man. He was gentle, kind, sweet, generous, and an all-around gentleman, and it pained my heart to learn it was built on a lie. All I wanted was to be with him because no other man would suffice.

When I grew tired of reminiscing, I sent him a text.

Sierra: Wyd?

As soon as I sat the phone down, he texted back.

Dre: In the hood

That meant he was posted with his boys doing absolutely nothing.

Sierra: Come feed me and the baby

I laughed when he sent me the eggplant emoji.

Sierra: You so nasty ☺
Dre: How? Ain't that's what you meant?
Sierra: Yes, but I want food, too
Dre: From where?
Sierra: Popeye's
Dre: U love that greasy-ass chicken
Sierra: That's what the baby wants
Dre: U not about to keep feeding my baby that unhealthy shit. This ur last time eating that
Sierra: Okay ☹
Dre: Where u at?
Sierra: Marriot in Plantation on 78th by the mall in room 516
Dre: What the fuck u doing there?
Sierra: Long story
Dre: I'll be there soon
Sierra: Come now. We hungry ☹
Dre: Okay I'm leaving now
Sierra: ☺

I smiled at the phone before placing it on my chest and hugging it like it was Dre. My body felt tingly all over since I knew he was on his way. He always had that effect on me. I didn't lose my virginity to him, but he was the second person I slept with, and he did some shit to me I didn't think was humanly possible. That was the reason my head was so gone and my nose was so open. He ruled my mind, body, and pussy with an iron dick, and it killed me on the inside knowing he fucked that ho like that.

Tokee didn't deserve Dre because she was so insecure and she was always on his back about any- and everything. No man wanted to be hounded by his girl day and night. Just give the nigga some space and he'll always come back home, but I guess nobody ever taught her that. He needed a woman who

134

could handle him. One who had his back, no matter what. I wouldn't dare argue with my man after he been out hustling all day. That's the last thing he wanna do. It's already bad he has to fight with the world on the outside, but to come home to part two with the one who's supposed to give him peace is crazy.

A notification came through my phone, and it was Dre telling me he would be here in 15 minutes. Apparently I wasted time lying in bed when I should've been getting ready for my visit.

I jumped up from the bed and made a beeline for the shower. There was no time to stay in long and take a Moses shower, so I made it quick. I poured some Pure Seduction shower gel onto my rag and cleansed my body. When I finished, I stepped from the shower and lotioned my body. I spent a little more time caressing my belly than I did the other parts. Having a baby was never something I planned on doing, being that I was staying in a group home. My life was never in order, so I knew kids were not something that should be included in my future.

In six months I would be giving birth to a human being I would be responsible for. That made me nervous all by itself, but I had some good people in my corner, so I wasn't worried one hundred percent.

After I was done, I slipped into my robe and walked to the door to see if my little bodyguard was out lurking the premises. Jamir told me earlier that he would be leaving because he had an errand to run, so I was hoping he left for that already.

"Jamir," I called out to him, but there was no answer. The door was cracked to the bedroom he slept in. Double-checking, I peeked inside and made sure it was empty. The last thing I needed was for him to be listening in on us. Corey knew he was over the top with this babysitting shit. It ain't like they were looking for me or knew where I was at, for that matter. All I wanted was for Barbee to be returned safely. I truly missed her, and Corey was losing his mind without her. He needed her, no doubt.

There was a knock on the door. My heart raced with anticipation, and between my legs was a throbbing sensation. With the door wide open, in front of me stood what could make my heart melt in the coldest weather. Dre stood at 5'11" with smooth Hershey skin covered in creative artwork, deep, dark waves that would drown a bitch, sparkling brown eyes that would hypnotize me, pearly white teeth, and juicy lips I loved to suck on. *Damn he has me mesmerized.* My baby daddy was fine.

"You gon' let me in, or we just gon' stand here undressing each other with our eyes?"

"Hush." Stepping to the side, I let him in. "My room to the right."

Watching him walk was an orgasm within itself, and I enjoyed the view. See, the gag is Dre is bowlegged, and he was hanging real low between his legs. Placing my food on the nightstand, he kicked his shoes off and got comfortable on the bed. That was my queue to lock the door and sashay over to my man. I hopped up on the bed and straddled him. The hunger I had for food was quickly replaced with a sexual hunger for Dre. I leaned forward and kissed him slowly. His hand was on the back of my neck while he reciprocated the kiss. Hot and horny was an understatement on how I was really feeling. My body yearned to be underneath him, taking every inch in my stomach while screaming his name.

Our kiss ended abruptly. "I thought you were hungry?"

"I am." Grabbing a handful of dick, I winked at him. "Hungry for this."

"We have plenty of time for that. Feed my baby first so he or she can go to sleep, and then I can put you to sleep."

"Okay." The way he talked to me turned me on.

Dre sat and watched me ingest all of my food until the box was empty. A burp followed shortly after. "Oh, excuse me."

"If you wasn't pregnant, I would call you nasty."

"Thanks for giving me a pass."

Dre stood up and removed his clothes. Watching closely, I paid special attention to his rock-hard phallus. I couldn't wait for him to slide that up in me. Grabbing my hands, he pulled me from the bed and untied my robe. Slipping it off my shoulders, it fell to the floor. Our lips connected, and our tongues danced slowly together. My breathing picked up, and my juices started to flow on the spot with no penetration. Dre eased me onto the bed gently and slid into my slippery goodness.

The way he made love to me was always passionate. He always took his time with my young, inexperienced body. I moaned loudly in his ear, rubbing his strong shoulders as he dipped in and out of me.

"Ah."

To silence me, he placed his mouth on top of mine, slipping his tongue in and kissing me hard. The volume of his dick – yes, length and width – was something I didn't ever think I could get used to. The way he dominated my small frame always had me squirming underneath his. Dre killed me every time we had sex, but I loved every minute of it. Thinking of how much I loved him brought tears to my eyes. They slid down the side of my face.

"Shit!" Dre hollered, still stroking. His body started to vibrate, and I knew he was coming inside of me, like he always did. From the time we started having sex, we never used a condom. Well, once would be more fitting, although he took it off in the middle of sex.

After it all came to an end, Dre pulled me close to him and wipe my tears with his thumb. "Why you crying?"

"You."

"What I did now?" Dre acted as if he didn't know he broke my heart more than once.

"You hurt me," I admitted.

"And I apologized. How many times do I have to say I'm sorry?"

"Sorry won't piece my heart back together." My voice cracked while I attempted to express my feelings to the man who brought on the pain in the first place. "You stomped all over my heart," I cried. "I love you, and you don't even care."

"Sierra." I could feel his cool breath on my face when he exhaled. Dre lifted my chin with his finger and looked me dead in my eyes. I braced myself, not knowing what he was about to say. My heart sped up. "I love you, too, and I've felt this way for a long time, but I didn't believe we could make it in a committed relationship with such a huge gap in our ages."

Sucking my teeth, I cut him off. "And why is that?"

"You so young, and you haven't experienced life yet. I'm much older than you, and I've done it all. I didn't want to lock you down like that. That would've made you rebellious, because you would probably get curious and see what you've been missing out, dealing with me."

"No. I only want to be with you. I don't want anyone else." Pleading my case was the only thing on my mind. Dre needed to know I planned on being loyal and faithful to only him.

"Our situation has changed, and I want to be here for you at all times, but I know Tokee ain't going for that."

Just hearing her name made me angry. "Fuck Tokee!" I screamed. "You gon' let her dictate when you can see me and your child?"

"Calm down, 'cause that's not what I meant."

"What is it, then?" He had to straighten me, because we would be in this bitch fighting, and he knew that.

"I can see you anytime, but we still live together, and we married. That would cause a lot of problems for me."

"Divorce her." The bluntness in my voice shook me.

"I thought about it."

"Don't think, do it."

"It's complicated."

"Yeah, right, and I don't believe you," I pouted.

"It's the truth, and I can't give you the details. But if I really cared about my marriage, do you think I would've brought her to the dinner? Or given you that much attention?" Tapping me on the side of the head, he continued. "Think about it. When I saw you at the wedding, I knew I made a mistake, seeing how much I hurt you. As you can see, I didn't curse you out, deny you, or put my hands on you. Instead, I tried to explain it to you."

"That's because my brother was there."

Dre laughed like I had just told him a funny joke. "Baby, I'm not scared of your brother. The only reason he getting a pass right now is because he has the upper hand on our relationship. We came from the same streets, and we bleed the same blood. There ain't a man alive that could put fear in my heart."

That last comment made me lean up on my arm. "How does he have control over our relationship?"

"I'm 25, and you 16. He can easily press charges and get me on statutory rape. If it wasn't for you and the love I have for you, he would've had to shoot me one. I'll play his game for now, but he don't have too many more times to try me."

"You feel comfortable threatening my brother in front of me?"

"What you gon' do?" he joked, squeezing my nose.

"Jump in it. You do know I can fight." Dre saw me strap with this chick at the group home I was in. I straight mutted that ho. That's why he don't want me to beat up Tokee.

"Yeah, jump in on my side."

"Nope."

"Cum thicker than blood, remember that."

"You must be crazy."

Dre kissed me once more before we cuddled up for a nap. Silence fell on us for a few minutes, but of course I had to break it, because now I had mixed feelings about everything he just said to me.

"What's gonna happen between us? Is this how it's gon' be?"

"I'll fix it."

"Promise me."

"I promise. Now, go to sleep."

Smiling from ear to ear, I closed my eyes like he said. I was happy, and for what it's worth, his promise was good enough for me, as long as he fulfilled it and didn't leave it empty. Dre gave me his word he was going to make things right between us, and I believed him. I had no reason to doubt his word. At the end of the day, that's all he had.

I squeezed him tighter and imagined what it would be like to go to sleep and wake up to him every morning. My time was coming, and I could feel it, but for now I was going to enjoy our moment together.

***

Corey

I slid the key into the slot and pushed the door open. When I walked in, it was too quiet for my liking, and the door was closed at that. I rushed over, trying to barge in, but the door was locked.

"If this nigga fucking my sister, I'ma kill his ass," I mumbling under my breath as I pulled out my heat. "Sierra!" I yelled while banging on the door.

When the door opened, she was looking stupid. "What the fuck y'all doing in here?" I screamed.

Dre pulled the cover from over his head. "Who the fuck is that?"

Apparently he was asleep, and I had just woken him with the screaming. I looked at Sierra. "Where is Jamir?"

"He said he had an errand to run, so he left." Sierra tilted her head and caught sight of my gun. "You though he was in here?"

"Yeah."

"That's why you have that gun in your hand?"

I tucked my gun away, but I didn't bother to respond to her and made my entrance into the room.

"Who is Jamir?" Dre asked.

"My babysitter," Sierra responded, because I wasn't answering shit.

Dre was the last face I expected to see. "What you doing here?"

"She was hungry, so I had to come and feed my babies."

The sarcasm dripped from his words, and I swear I wanted to cap this nigga in the chest. I looked toward the nightstand and saw the Popeye's box. "Yeah, that ain't all you fed her. You had to fuck this nigga so he can bring you something to eat?"

"Corey, stop," Sierra shouted. "Why you doing all of that?"

From the corner of my eye, I saw Dre pulling up his pants and walking toward me, so I turned my attention. "'Cause this nigga married, and when he hurt you, who you think gon' be there to pick up the pieces?"

Dre stood a few feet away from me, careful not to come into my personal space. He rubbed his hands together like he wanted to square up. "I see you have a lot of animosity toward me."

"You know I do."

"Yo' sister ain't gotta fuck me for food. I'm gon' feed her regardless. Not only did you insult me, but you insulted her, and that shit ain't cool. Now, I'm feeling some type of way about that. You can come at me all day, I don't give a fuck, but she don't deserve that from her own brother. You worried about me hurting her, but that's what you doing."

The look on Sierra's face hurt me bad, and I couldn't say shit because he was right, although I hated to admit it.

I walked over to her. "I'm sorry for what I said." She nodded her head. "But you need to listen to me. This is a married man you fucking. Where you think he going when he leave here? Home, to his wife, while you here by yourself. When that baby come, you gon' find out that baby won't keep him."

"See, here we go again. We was cool until you found out I was messing with your sister."

I let go of Sierra. "I don't want my sister fucking with you, period."

"You don't know how I feel about your sister, and I'll never leave her alone to raise our baby. Hate it or love it, but I got her for the next 18 years."

The grin on his face made me up my strap on his ass. Dre didn't flinch. "Don't pull it if you ain't prepared to pull the trigger," he said coolly.

Sierra screamed, distracting me and causing me to look in her direction. "No, Corey. I love him, and he loves me, too."

A black shadow caught my attention. I swiveled my head back to Dre, and he had his gun pulled out, aiming at my chest. "What you wanna do? We can end this shit right now, and she won't have baby daddy or a brother."

It was a real deal showdown going on right in front of my sister. I never wanted her to see me in action like this, but he tried it.

Sierra was bawling her eyes out. "Stop, please! Don't do this."

Dre and I were from the same streets, and we ran together, but that shit came to an end once their relationship came to the light. I know he didn't know about her, but I didn't care. The fact of the matter was he was too old for her, and he knew that. The last time we were in a situation like this was when we ran down on some niggas, but we were on the same side. This time we were on opposite sides. Rivals. We both knew what type of damage we could cause, and that made our actions unpredictable. No one made a move. Our eyes were locked in on each other, and our breathing was steady. Sierra's whimpers could be heard, but I ignored them, and so did Dre.

"Corey, put the gun down, please. He's my baby's father. Please."

I didn't give a fuck whose daddy he was, this nigga tried it. I wasn't putting my strap down.

"Dre, baby, please put the gun down. That's my brother."

She was tired of being ignored, so she stepped in the middle of both guns. Dre's gun was directly on her chest.

"Move, Sierra," Dre demanded.

"Not until you put the gun down."

I watched him watch her. Dre stood there for a minute, eyeing her, but the way he looked at her was the same way I looked at Barbee. That made me wonder if he really did love my sister.

"I'll stand right here since I'm the problem between you two. If you really love me like you say you do, you will put the gun down for me."

Dre thought for a minute before he slowly released the grip on his gun and brought his arm down. Sierra hugged him and cried in his arms.

"I'm sorry, baby," Dre apologized to her and tossed his gun onto the bed. That made me put my gun down as well. I tucked it back into my waistband and walked out of the room.

My mind was racing, and I felt like I was losing it. First it was Barbee, now this. He really took me there, and I had to deal with this nigga for the rest of my life, as long as they had this child together. My adrenaline was pumping hard and I needed someone to take my frustrations out on, and I guess he was an easy target because he was here. To hear my sister beg for his life really did something to me, and I knew I couldn't kill him because of her. She would never forgive me if I forced her to be a single parent. I came to the conclusion that as long as he didn't make her cry, I wouldn't kill him.

I left the hotel room in deep thought, contemplating my next move.

Chapter 12

Rich

Rolling over in the middle of the afternoon and seeing Barbee's face was heaven-sent. She looked like an angel as she slept so peacefully. Her snores were soft and like sensual music to my ears. It reminded me of the jazz music I listened to whenever I needed to calm down.

I guess she could feel my eyes piercing her soul. Barbee stirred in her sleep, then her eyes fluttered a little before she opened them completely. Barbee looked underneath the covers to see if she was naked.

"Why are you staring at me?" she asked.

"You look so beautiful when you sleep."

She sat up in the bed and rubbed her face with her hands. "Ugh. I have a headache."

"That's 'cause you had too much to drink and too much fun with your little boyfriend last night."

Barbee rolled her eyes at me, like I cared, and climbed out of bed to go to the bathroom. Pulling down her dress, she looked back at me. "I know you took advantage of me."

I licked my lips, savoring her delicious juices she left behind just hours earlier. "That was consensual, baby."

Just as she closed the bathroom door, my cellphone rang. I thought it was Michelle, and I was not in the mood for her bickering today. Thankfully, it was Mattie.

"Yeah."

"I'm afraid I have some bad news."

"And what could that possibly be?"

"I found my uncle dead at the mansion."

What he said to me just didn't make sense. There was no way Giovanni could be dead. "Stop bullshittin'."

"No bullshit," he huffed into the phone. "I wish I was."

"What, he had a heart attack or some shit?"

"He was murdered. The police been at the mansion for hours. Consuela and John are dead, too."

"Damn, that just fucked me up."

"Shit, me too, but I need you to meet me at the restaurant in 30 minutes."

"I'm on the way."

After I hung up the phone, I sat there trying to figure out what the fuck was going on. Giovanni was like a father to me, and he always treated me like a son, despite the fact he thought I had something to do with what Barbee did. We were going to get to the bottom of his murder, and whoever did it was going to pay with their very own life, and maybe a few family members. Giovanni was the reason I was on top. From the time I met him, he had always been there for me. The only thing I didn't like was the fact he shot Barbee and killed our baby. That was the reason I couldn't let him know I had found her. I couldn't let him kill her, father or not.

Barbee finally came out of the bathroom.

"I have to go, but I'll be back soon."

"I'll be here when you get back. Don't worry." Obviously she didn't catch my drift since she went back to bed, pulling the covers over her head.

I quickly pulled them back. "I'm sorry, but I have to take you back down to the basement until I get back."

She frowned. "Are you serious right now?"

"I'm sorry, but yes, I'm serious."

Barbee threw the covers off of her, upset with my decision to treat her like a prisoner. Just because she had good pussy and I was hitting that didn't mean I was going to be stupid. Barbee was a clever chick, and I couldn't risk losing the upper hand. She wasn't happy at the moment, but I would make it up to her later. Barbee didn't understand that I was only trying to spare her life. If she tried to escape, I knew things could get really bad for her. She had no clue the type of man I was or the damage I could do. She didn't follow directions too well, and I didn't want to hurt her, or kill her, for that matter. I'm talking *capital punishment!*

When I pulled up to the restaurant, there were several cars in the parking lot. Normally when I met him there it was empty, meaning closed for business in order for us to have privacy. "This nigga off his rocker," I mumbled while strolling to the entrance.

To my surprise, the closed sign was in the window. "I guess he ain't off his rocker, after all."

I tapped on the window and waited for one of his little goons to let me in. Stepping inside, I dapped everyone up and took a seat at one of the tables. There were six of us in attendance.

"Where is Mattie?" I asked Mattie's right-hand man.

"He stepped away to drain the lizard," he laughed.

"I didn't need to know all of that. All you had to say was he stepped away for a moment."

There was a lot of chatter amongst the group, but that quickly came to an end when Mattie walked into the room. I laughed out loud, grabbing everybody's attention.

"What's funny?" Mattie asked, while walking toward me.

"These niggas," I pointed them out. "They stopped talking when you reappeared, like you Al Pacino or some shit." Mattie and I slapped hands.

"I am," he laughed. "What the fuck you talking about?"

"You wish you was that nigga."

"I'm working on it." Focusing on the group, he spoke, "Alright, now we can get to the point of this meeting."

This nigga really thought shit was sweet between us since Giovanni was dead. I hoped he didn't think I'd forgot about him pulling that gun on me back at the mansion. For now it was cool, and I was gonna play my position until I got myself acquainted with the dope connect. After that went down, it was lights out for this nigga.

"As you all know, my uncle was murdered, along with Consuela and John. It wasn't a robbery because there was nothing missing from the house, but I'm still looking into it. Meanwhile, so are the police. That means they will be looking into his finances and assets. That means we have to lay low for a while until this whole thing blows over. If you hear anything about the murder, let me know. Just don't move on it without talking to me. We can't afford to bring attention to ourselves." Mattie paced the floor with his hands in his pockets. "That also means we can't move any dope. I'm trying to get something worked out with the connect my uncle dealt with, but he's a little sketchy about us being a liability."

Those were definitely not the words I wanted to hear, and apparently no one else, for that matter. A loud outburst could be heard, along with heavy grunts.

"I'm pissed," Mattie tried to explain, "but we all should have money stashed away for emergencies, because this is one of them. Once I get the word, I'll let everyone know the deal."

Mattie turned his back to us, and that was my cue to leave. My mind was racing trying to think of a plan, because I wasn't about to sit around and not make any money. There were so many ideas crowding my brain.

Then I came up with the perfect plan.

When I made it back to the Bunny Ranch, I went to the basement to get Barbee and bring her upstairs. She was still mad about earlier, but she would be okay. The proposal I was about to hit her with was going to make her very happy.

"Baby," I called out to her, but she ignored me. I kept talking anyway. "I have some good news for you."

She looked up. "You letting us go?"

Barbee was so hopeful I could see it in her eyes. "No, but you're close."

"Well, you don't have good news," she said nastily.

Her attitude was about to make me snap, but I decided to give her a pass. "I've been thinking about what you said, and I'm going to take you up on your offer."

There was a sparkle in her eye, and she actually smiled. That was the happiest she's been since she's been here. "You're letting my sister go?"

"Under two conditions, though."

"What?" She was skeptical.

"We hit a lick tonight, and she's free in the morning."

"And what's the second condition?"

"You stay here with me and work off your debt to Giovanni in exchange for your life. He wants to kill you, but I'm not going to let that happen. As long as we get this money back to him, he'll let it go."

"That's a lot of money to repay," she said sadly.

"It is, but this is the price you have to pay." I looked at her closely so she could feel where I was coming from. "You have a decision to make, life or death. I'm cool with either one."

Barbee thought about what I said for a hot second. "Okay, I'll do it."

Later on that night, we went to another club in Dade. This time there was no intended target, so she needed to really work her magic. As usual, I was ducked off in the corner keeping my eyes on everything moving, and sipping on my drink. I was hoping this wasn't going to be a long night like last time.

To my surprise, Barbee was heading to the door just as that thought left my head. My prayers had been answered. I knew God looked out for the hustlers, too.

Downing the rest of my drink, I followed closely as she walked through the parking lot. I guess freeing her sister was her only motivation. I trailed the car until they reached their destination.

***

Barbee

Being held captive was something I never saw in the cards for me, and after I left Fox alone, I never thought I would be forced to do this again. Rich easily brought that to life for me, but if he didn't have Mercedes, he would've never made it this far. I was only doing this to keep my sister alive. She was the only one I had left. Rich knew he had me in a compromising position, so his intentions were to milk me until the end, mentally, physically, and sexually. To keep her alive, I'd rob Jesus and ask for forgiveness later.

Here I was once again, riding in the car with another target in exchange for my sister's freedom. Sitting at the red light, my mind begin to wander. Rich wanted this robbery to be different, and I couldn't help but wonder why,

Tony, my target, was drunk, and it wasn't a normal drunk, either. He was one of those aggressive drunks, and that was too much for me. I lost count at how many times I had to move his hand from my thigh. Tony had money, but he was far from attractive, and that made my job that much harder. Being a little

anyone to watch you when I step out." Rich took the phone from my hand. "Now, do we have an understanding?"

I nodded my head yes. My mood changed quickly, and I wanted to cry so badly, but I needed to be strong and figure out a way to overcome this new obstacle I was just faced with. Rich and I walked down to the basement, and Mercedes was so happy to see me.

"Are you okay?" she asked.

"Yes," I lied, trying to keep my composure.

"Aye," Rich shouted, causing the both of us to look up. "Give them some privacy." He was talking to his cousin, the babysitter.

I waited until they left to talk. "This is what's about to happen." I paused and fought back every tear trying to slip through the cracks. "Rich is going to let you go, but on one condition only."

"What's that?" Mercedes asked. I could hear the concern in her voice.

My head hung low, and I looked at the floor. I couldn't look her in the eyes and say it. "I have to stay here and work off the debt for that work we stole from Giovanni in exchange for our lives."

"Barbee, no! How do you know he won't kill you after you have worked the debt off?"

"That's a chance I have to take. I can't afford to lose you, too."

"But I might lose you."

It broke my heart to hear the hurt in her voice. When I looked up at her, there were tears in her eyes. "You won't lose me. I promise." I wiped her face with my hand. "I'm going to make it out alive. I have a plan in place that's going to set me free."

"What if he kills you?"

"He won't. Rich is weak when it comes to me. Trust me, if he wanted me dead, he would've killed me already. This is what I need you to do." I squeezed her hand in mine and sucked up the tears. "You can't tell anyone where I am, Mercedes, and you can't call the police or he will kill me. If anyone asks, just tell them you went away to clear your head about Nehiya, and you haven't heard from me since that day."

"Okay."

"Promise me you won't, please," I begged.

"I promise."

"I'll be back. I'm going to get Rich so you can get out of here."

I stood up and walked away to find my captor. My feet moved slowly, as if a ball and chain were connected and I was taking my final walk on death row. The thoughts in my head were everywhere, and I had a feeling I was going to be here for a very long time. Rich made it that much harder for me to get away from his crazy-ass.

After walking the green mile, I found him and his cousin sitting in the living room, talking. "It's done."

"Okay," he replied and stood up to approach me. "Let's go free her so we can carry on with our lives."

Rich untied Mercedes' hands. "Turn that bomb off," she panicked.

"It's off," he replied before removing the final piece of rope tied around her body. "He's gonna take you back to your car, and you know what to do from there, right?"

"Yes," she replied. Mercedes knew what he meant by that.

Mercedes stood up, came to where I was standing, and gave me a hug. I squeezed her tight and whispered in her ear. "Please do what I asked you to do."

"I won't say anything. I promise."

The grip I had on her was so tight I was sure she would suffocate of I didn't let her go. "I love you, Mercedes, and I'll see you soon." I finally allowed my tears to flow freely. This moment was bittersweet, and I wasn't sure if I would ever see her again.

"Promise me."

"I promise."

"Okay, let's break up the family reunion, unless you wanna stay. We have work to do."

I never thought Rich could be so insensitive and cruel, but that showed how much I knew about him. I was sure it was because he hadn't taken his meds.

We finally let go, and just like that, she was gone.

As soon as I made it back to the bedroom I lay down, curled up like a baby, and cried my eyes out. I felt as if the world had finally come to an end. Since the day I left Fox alone, I had always called the shots on whatever I did, but now I was marching to the beat of someone else's drum. Rich made me feel powerless and helpless. I was trapped, and there was nothing I could do about it. He had complete control over me.

Destiny Skai

Chapter 13

Rich

Barbee was upset. I stood in the hallway next to the room door, and I could hear her cries. Deep down inside there was still a soft spot in my heart for her, although she had plans on crossing me in the first place. *Damn, she fuckin' with me right now!* I wanted to walk away, but my concrete shoes were keeping me in place. Or maybe it was heart weighing me down to the floor.

My phone vibrated in my pocket, so I pulled it out. *Ugh!* It was Michelle. I was not in the mood for her interrogation. I took a few steps backward away from the door so Barbee couldn't hear me.

"Hello."

"What are you doing?" she asked.

"Working."

"Well, you need to come home. I don't know what you been doing, but you need to get here," she demanded.

Yeah I hadn't been home, but she needed to leave me the fuck alone. "I'm out here trying to get money for our family. Did you forget another baby is on the way?"

"You knew that shit."

"I'll be there."

"Now, Rich."

Michelle hung up on me. I could see I was gon' have to put her ass in her place when I got there. I kept telling her that her face ain't pregnant and I'd make her swallow her teeth.

I went back to the door and peeked in at Barbee. She had stopped crying, so I walked into the room. Her eyes were closed, so I assumed she was sleeping. I tiptoed from the room and grabbed my keys before I hit the front door. I wasn't worried about her doing anything because the ball was in my court.

On my way home, my ideas were on heavy rotation. More than likely we would be working tonight, but I believed we needed to give Miami a break for a few weeks. We had two successful hits, and I wanted to keep it that way. There was no need to make the block hot when we didn't have to. The only problem was Palm Beach was too risky. I couldn't risk anyone seeing us together. Our best bet would be to go a little bit further and avoid my territory. Maybe we would go out of town and hit a lick or two, then come back home. Whatever decision I made was going to be soon, and I would know by the time night fell.

I pulled up in my driveway and took a deep breath. All Michelle wanted to do was argue, fuck, and take my money, but I didn't want to do either. When she got pregnant, she made me strap up afterward. She said she didn't trust my black ass, and she wasn't about to risk me bringing her back any diseases. It was funny because she would never leave me.

I got out of the car with the book bag full of money. I put my key in the door, and it opened up without me doing anything else, like she was waiting on me.

There stood an angry Michelle with her hand out. "You know what time it is," she snapped. "Pay to play."

I reached into the bag and pulled out the $1,000 I put to the side for her. I attempted to place it in her hand, but she snatched it and thumbed through the bills.

"That's not enough."

I reached back into the bag and pulled another $1,000 and passed it to her. This time she walked away.

"Bitch," I mumbled under my breath so she couldn't hear me. Michelle wasn't dumb. She knew what time it was with me.

160

The kids were in their rooms still asleep. I didn't understand why she let them stay up late and sleep so late. They slept like they worked night jobs and paid bills. Normally I would wake them up, but I wanted to lay down and relax.

I went into the bathroom and took a long piss. It felt like I had been drinking all night and held it until morning. After I washed my hands, I went into the room and stripped all the way down to my boxers and lay down. Michelle couldn't wait to lie next to me and start with the foolery.

"Who is she?"

"Who is who?" I asked, playing dumb.

"The new bitch that has you out day and night."

"I've been working. I told you that already."

"And you think I believe you?"

"It's not about what you believe, it's about what you can prove."

Michelle huffed and puffed. I guess she didn't like my response. "Listen, this is getting old, and I can see you are never gon' stop. I tell you what, though: if you don't, I will leave you and take the kids with me."

"You ain't taking my kids no-goddam-where, so shut up talking that crazy shit."

"I'm serious, Rich. I'm not taking my new baby through this bullshit with you. As long as you not fucking another bitch, you work and come home."

"I ain't doing shit."

"Yes, you are, and you're sloppy with it. I can always tell when you found your latest toy to play with. Do you even tell these girls you're married?"

I ignored her and hummed nothing in particular, just to tune her out.

"Answer me!" she yelled.

"Bitch, I had a bad day. I ain't trying to hear that shit," I laughed, antagonizing her.

Michelle slapped me across the face. "You better watch your mouth."

"I keep telling you, your mouth ain't pregnant, so you better stop talking to me crazy." I rolled over on her ass and tried to get some sleep.

In the midst of me getting a nap, I could feel something warm on me, and it felt good. I even moaned and grunted a few times, but I didn't open my eyes. This dream was better than reality at the moment. My body started to rock, and I rubbed my chest. Then I eased my hand down to my boxers, but they were missing. I felt a body on top of me, and that's when I finally opened my eyes. Michelle was on top of me, grinding on my dick with her eyes closed.

"Ah," she moaned.

She had a lot of nerve, but I participated. Gripping her hips, I pushed up inside of her so she could feel every inch of me. Her belly was in the way of me pulling her close to me so I could really dig in it. Every thrust I made, she made it with me. I smacked her on the ass a few times, and a minute later I was cumming.

Michelle didn't waste any time climbing off of me and cleaning herself up. I lay there staring at the ceiling until I felt a warm liquid tickle my skin. When I looked down, the semen from the condom was making its way to freedom. I got up and went to the bathroom. Sliding the condom off, I dropped it into the toilet and took a piss. *Woo, what a relief!* I stood there with my head back and eyes closed, enjoying the sensation. When it was all over, I flushed the toilet and turned on the water in the shower before I stepped in.

The Fetti Girls 2

The hot water hit my skin and opened up my pores. The steam filled my nostrils and cleared my nasal passages. My body was covered in suds, but they soon started to vanish when the droplets of water collided with my skin. I turned the water off, and I felt rejuvenated, like I had just washed away my sins. Pulling the towel from the metal towel rack, I stepped out and dried off. Wrapping the towel around my waist, I walked over to the sink to brush my teeth and gargle. Looking into the mirror, I was happy with my smile, so I turned off the light and went back into the room to get dressed.

"Where are you going?" Michelle asked as I put on a pair of boxers.

"Back to work," I replied, slipping into a pair of jeans.

"Don't you mean 'back to her?'"

"Michelle, you can say whatever you like. You got your money, so do what you do best and go out and spend it. Spare me the extra questions and shit."

"You are such a bastard."

"Tell me something I don't know."

Michelle rolled over and did what she did best: pout. Now was not the time to play this bullshit-ass game with her. I had money to get and a bad bitch working to get it. She could get mad all she wanted to, 'cause she ain't gon' do shit.

I pulled my tank top over my head and sat down to put on my shoes. A few seconds passed, and I stood up and picked up my belongings. I walked through the house for the final time, and my kids were still in bed. I shook my head and walked to the front door so I could leave.

As soon as I stepped out onto the porch, the sun knocked the wind out of me. It was so damn hot I started sweating immediately. I walked briskly to the car, unlocked the doors, and got inside. Revving up the engine, I turned on the air conditioner quickly and gave myself a moment to catch my breath.

Tonight was going to be a great night. I hoped. I wanted to hit it big, and not just for a few grands, either. Barbee was gon' have to step her game up.

***

Corey

Each day without my queen was driving me insane. I couldn't think straight, and I was on the verge of catching a fuckin' case because of it. This nigga Rich was gon' have to see me soon. I knew he had my most prized possession in his presence, and ain't no telling what he was doing to her. Just the thought of him touching or fucking her was getting to me mentally. She used to fuck this nigga, so I knew it was a possibility. There was also no telling if she went willingly and made this shit look good, 'cause apparently she was fucking us around the same time. People lie, phone records and text messages don't. One thing I knew for a fact was everything done in the dark would come to the light. She portrayed this innocent and faithful persona, but she was far from that. I knew she was sneaky, conniving, and a fuckin' master manipulator, but I never thought she would try and play me like that. I thought we were better than that, but in all honesty, how well did I really know her?

Sitting up on the couch, I stretched and reached for my cup of Patron. This was my third cup, and it wasn't helping me think rationally for one second. But they do say a drunk person speaks a sober mind, and that was me right now. I took a sip of my drink and sat it back down, then I reached for the blunt in the ashtray. Picking up the lighter, I lit the end of it, put it to my lip, and took a hard pull. The potency of the weed was so strong I coughed a few times.

"Shit!"

I thought I was about to choke to death in this bitch. That Crip was no joke. Two puffs was all I needed, so I put it back in the ashtray. A loud melody caused me to look in the direction of my phone. I leaned up and lifted my shirt a little, 'cause it was keeping me from moving. When I picked up the phone and looked at the screen, it was a number I didn't recognize. My heart skipped a beat, and I immediately thought it was Barbee.

"Hello?"

"Corey?" she asked.

"Who is this?"

"Mercedes. Are you home?"

"Yeah, why?"

"I need to talk to you about Barbee. Can I stop by?"

"Yeah." My response was nonchalant, but I couldn't front about being anxious to hear what she had to say. The alcohol gave me so many scenarios to consider. The problem was I didn't know which direction I should take. Hopefully Mercedes would be able to shed some light on the situation.

"I'll be there in 30 minutes."

"Okay."

After hanging up the phone, I tossed it on the couch beside me. The suspense was eating me alive. The fact she appeared so calm signaled to me that maybe Barbee wasn't in great danger, or any danger for that matter. Since this ordeal occurred, my feelings were beginning to shift in a different direction, and it wasn't for the better. I was starting to think that proposing to her was probably a mistake. The text messages kept popping up in my mind, and all I could focus on was the fact she cheated. As of right now, I was the only faithful one in the relationship.

An hour had passed, and I was about to slide when Mercedes called me back.

"Yeah."

"I'm outside."

Slowly, I pulled myself from the couch and stretched. This was the moment I had been waiting on. Walking over to the door, I removed the new lock I had recently installed and opened the door. Mercedes was standing there with a tear-stained face. I panicked right off the bat. *This can't be good!* My breathing was a little heavier, and my heart raced with anticipation.

"Come in."

Mercedes wasn't herself. When she walked past me, I caught a whiff of her odor. It was like the sun mixed with sweat. Like she hadn't had a bath in days, and her hair was disheveled. This wasn't like her.

"Have a seat." I pointed to the sofa across from me while I went back to my original spot. "So, what's up?"

"I don't know how to say this, or if I should be saying anything."

I held my hand up, not giving her a chance to go any further. "Why you here if you not sure about saying something?"

"It's difficult."

"Fuck you mean, it's difficult?" My voice boomed, causing Mercedes to jump backward instinctively. She played with her keys and avoided eye contact with me. At this point I didn't have time for the bullshit, and she could go back to wherever the fuck she came from with the games. My forehead drew wrinkles, and my face was scrunched up. If she knew better, she would get to the point of this fuckin' visit. "If you ain't gon' tell me what's up, then you can haul ass. I'm not with the shit." I stood up and walked over to the door, placing my hand on the knob.

"Okay, wait. Please," she cried.

"Talk." I moved my hand, but I stayed by the door.

"Barbee was kidnapped by this dude named Rich. He kidnapped me, too, but he let me go today." Mercedes' eyes were glued to the floor, while she continued to play with her keys. "She begged me not to say anything."

Now I was confused. "So, why are you telling me?"

"I'm scared for her, Corey. He might kill her."

"Why the fuck would she tell you not to say anything?"

Mercedes sniffled. "She had to agree to stay and work for him in order to let me go."

I just looked at this muthafucka like she was stupid and shook my head. Then she finally looked up.

"You don't care about what happens to her?"

"Forgive me for not being concerned, but this sounds like bullshit."

"I swear it's the truth. She was crying and said she will get away from him soon. Corey, you've got to help her. Rich said she couldn't leave until she earned back the money from the product we took from Giovanni."

Suddenly, I became dizzy and could see stars. My knees felt weak, so I eased my way back to the couch. It finally made sense. The huge lump in my throat made it impossible for me to speak. All I could do was sit and stare. I knew one day this shit would come back and haunt us.

"They even killed Nehiya." A plethora of tears flooded her face as she rocked in her seat. "He was keeping us in a basement, but then he made her sleep upstairs with him. I don't know how much longer she's gonna make it, Corey. You have to find her."

The anger I felt toward her was replaced with rage, and I wanted to kill this nigga bad. I stood up and walked over to where she was sitting and sat down beside her. I placed my arm around her and patted her on the shoulder. "I'm going to find her and bring her back. Where is he keeping her?"

"I don't know," she sobbed. I was sure snot and tears were going to be on my shirt, but I let it slide.

"How you don't know if you were there with her?"

"His cousin blindfolded me and made me lay down in the front seat. And when Rich brought me there, I was tipsy, and he took a bunch of back roads. I'm not familiar with that area. I'm sorry." Mercedes continued to cry.

"It's gon' be okay. We're gonna find her."

"She said we can't call the police, either."

"Oh, don't worry, I won't. We gon' handle this shit on our own. I'm gon' call Amon so we can put a plan in motion. In the meantime, go home and clean yourself up. I'll call and check on you later."

Mercedes nodded her head and stood up with her things in her hands. She followed behind me until we were at the front door. There was no pep in her step, so I watched her walk through the parking lot until she made it to her car and pulled off.

Chapter 14

Barbee

Rolling over on my back, I had just awakened from a much-needed nap. Using my left hand to cover my mouth while I yawned, I used the other to wipe the crust from my eyes. I was too tired and drained from all that crying. Looking up at the ceiling, I would've never predicted this would be my deck of cards in life. *Is this karma or some shit?* All I knew was I had to beat Rich at his own game by finessing his ass. I got up to clean my face, because those would be the last tears I cried. On God! Whomever was praying on my downfall was winning at the moment, but I was about to turn that shit around. I was too savage to have the tables turned around on me. This shit had to stop.

Tossing my rag into the sink, I turned on the hot water until it reached the top. I rung it out and placed it onto my face. The steam from it opened my pores and seeped into my skin. It was very refreshing. Too bad I didn't have my exfoliating face scrub with me, so this would have to do for now. I placed my rag back onto the rack and walked back into the bedroom and sat on the bed. Staying indoors and in bed all day was not my style. I was a go-getter, and I wasn't used to sitting around. A brinks truck never came to my front door and dropped off any cash. I had to get out and get it by any means.

Five minutes had passed before I heard the front door close, followed by footsteps coming down the hallway. Rich walked in with this stupid-ass grin on his face.

"I see you're up?"

"I see you're a smart, yet observant man," I said sarcastically while avoiding eye contact. My focus was on my toes that were in need of a pedicure, not stupid questions that didn't deserve answers.

"Does everything out your mouth have to be slick?" He sat down on the bed and touched my knee, but I moved it. I didn't want his filthy-ass hands on me. "Can't we be friends to make our work go a little bit smoother?"

"Gee, Rich, that's kind of hard, being nice to the mutha-fucka that's keeping me against my will."

"Damn, you act like a nigga holding you hostage or some shit. A nigga letting you walk around freely."

"Maybe you should pick up a Webster."

"What the fuck is that?" he asked, questioning me as if I was the slow one. This made me second-guess the fact he wanted to work with kids. I wasn't sure he would be a good role model if he couldn't point them in the direction of a damn dictionary.

"Fuck it, Rich. Just Google it." I swear the man was acting like a ditzy-ass broad.

"See, if you would've stayed with me, I would've made an honest woman out of you. I would've fucked that hood shit right up out cha."

My lips curled up like I had just smelled something foul. "First of all, you wasn't gon' do shit to me. This my fuckin' mouth, and I talk how I want to."

Rich blinked long and hard, then rubbed his hand over his mouth. "Normally I would wire a bitch mouth shut with all that slick wrap, but today I'ma let you slide."

Suddenly the front door slammed shut, and both of us jumped on instinct. Rich took his gun out and aimed it at the door with his finger pressed slightly on the trigger. Whoever it was, they were on the verge of getting blasted with no questions. Rich gave me the side-eye, placing one finger over his lips, indicating I needed to be quiet.

Twenty seconds later a woman walked in, and she was very much pregnant.

Rich lowered his gun immediately and placed it at his side. He knew exactly who she was. She glanced at me for a brief second, shook her head, then focused on Rich. I guess she was checking out my attire, which consisted of a boyfriend tee and shorts.

"It's not what I believe, but what I can prove, right?"

Rich took a deep breath and his eyes fluttered. He was truly annoyed by her presence. "What the fuck you doing here, Michelle?"

I smirked because I just knew she was about to cause a real problem in here. As long as she didn't talk that shit in my direction, she was good. However, I was curious to know the nature of their relationship. Judging by her appearance, I guessed it was safe to say she was his baby mama. That meant he was fucking us around the same time, and apparently he was still hitting that. Why else would she pop up here? *Shit, he was still fucking me now!* I sat back and waited for the drama to unfold.

"Well, I needed to see who was keeping my husband away from his wife and kids," she stated with confidence while rubbing her beach-ball belly.

"Married?" I blurted out. That shit caught me by surprise, and I refused to let him get off the hook so easily. Just think, this muthafucka had the nerve to give me grief over leaving him and kidnapped me when he had kids and a wife at home. This bitch-ass nigga has a whole family out here, and he slangin' dick like he single. There was one thing I didn't like, and that was 'community dick.' I wasn't with that sharing shit. I'm stingy like Ginuwine.

"Yes, married," Michelle snapped. "Don't act like you didn't know."

I let her little snide remark slide off my back like water on a duck's ass, 'cause I would whoop this bitch's ass, pregnant and all. I didn't give several fucks.

"Michelle, now is not the time or place for this. We can discuss this at home, in private. I'm working right now, and you fucking it up."

"You call this work?" She pointed her chipped-polish fingertip at me. "It looks like you fucking this bitch right now."

"I will meet you at home when I'm done."

"No, muthafucka, you don't have a home after this." She looked at me again. "She's pretty and young, just like you like 'em. Young, home-wrecking bitches." She laughed. "He has four kids at home that you're keeping him from."

This bitch pushed my last button. I was trying to be mature about the situation, but my inner petty said *make this ho cry.* "First of all, I ain't wreck shit, and I ain't keeping him from nobody. I don't want your trifling-ass husband. You can take his ass with you." I hopped off the bed and pointed my finger in her direction. Rich made his way over to us in a hurry and stood in the middle. "You better watch yo' muthafuckin' mouth coming at me sideways, ho, before I show you what time it is."

"B, chill."

"You gon' let her talk to me like that?" Michelle slapped Rich across the face. He sucked it up and placed his hands on her shoulders.

"Stop it, and just go home. I'll explain everything when I get there, 'cause right now you blowing shit out of proportion."

"I can't believe you," she cried, bringing down the tone in her voice. She moved his hands off of her.

That was just like a soft-ass ho to start some shit and then cry when shit gets real. She realized I wasn't soft, and she had me fucked up.

"Every year it's the same shit with you: a new bitch. And I'm sick of it." Michelle took off her ring and sat it on the dresser. "This marriage is over, so don't come back home. I refuse to be an accessory to another one of your crimes."

Just as she pivoted on her heels, Rich grabbed her by her arm and snatched her back. "You better watch what the fuck you say, 'cause you skating on thin muthafuckin' ice." The anger he suppressed was out in the open. "Now, take that ring and take yo' ass home."

Michelle stood there unfazed by his threats. "You heard what I said. It's over." Before she walked out of the room, she glanced at me once more. "Go home. I'm sure your family misses you." Rich opened his mouth to speak, but she held up her hand to stop him. "I'm leaving, and if something happens to her, don't you fuckin' call me. Find you another alibi."

Michelle stormed out as if Rich was chasing her. I had never seen a pregnant woman move that fast, carrying a load so big. Silly-ass Rich looked me up and down before he walked out behind her seconds later.

With Michelle's words dangling in my ear, all I could hear was her saying, *'Go home. I know your family misses you.'* I couldn't fathom why she would say that. Just when I thought it couldn't get any worse, it did. The thing that bothered me the most was the fact she specifically stated that if something happened to me, he shouldn't call her for an alibi. I was mentally disturbed. I didn't have a PhD, but I was certain she was insinuating he killed before, and I had the potential to become his next victim. Not on my watch, though.

***

Corey

The bomb Mercedes dropped on me had a nigga bewildered. I would be lying if I said I didn't care, because moments ago I was thinking all types of shit. This dilemma was fucking with me bad. My number one goal was to get her home safe and sound, and after that she had some explaining to do. Barbee meant the world to me, but I was hurting. I truly felt I was going to need some space away from her. That would be in the best interest for both of us. The way I was feeling right then could ruin me and Amon's friendship and get me a year and a day in the Department of Corrections' custody. I had too much to lose, so getting away from her was my best move.

The generic ringtone to my burner phone rang, so I got up from the couch to get it off the kitchen counter. I picked it up quickly.

"Hello."

"Hi, this is Michelle Gathers. Is this Special Agent Stanley Burress?"

"Yes, it is, ma'am. How can I help you?"

"I have information on that missing girl you asked about earlier. I think I saw her."

My heart started to beat hard like some bass drums. "Are you sure you saw her?"

"I remember faces well, and I'm certain I saw her," Michelle assured me.

"Okay, I can meet you in about 45 minutes."

"Don't come to my house. Can you meet me at the Target on Palm Beach Lakes Boulevard?"

Something was up if she didn't want to meet at her house again. Maybe she decided to drop the dime on her husband after all. Whatever it was, I was grateful for it. "Yeah, I can meet you there. I'll call you when I'm close by."

"Okay."

"See you soon."

After we hung up, I called Amon right away. As soon as the phone stopped ringing, I started talking. I didn't give him a chance to say hello. "Aye, bruh, come to my house now," I shouted anxiously.

"What's going on?"

"It's about B, but I'll tell you when you get here."

"Give me 20 minutes."

"Yeah."

This was the call I had been waiting on. In a few hours Barbee would be back home, and my mind would be at ease. I would finally be able to sleep in my bed. Ever since she went missing, I wasn't able to sleep in there. The couch had become my best friend. I hadn't spoken to Sierra since I left the hotel, but I would make sure I checked on her just to make sure she was okay. I was still pissed off at the fact she was still sleeping with Dre's punk-ass. I didn't give a fuck how much he said he loved and cared for her. I didn't see it. If he felt like that, he would've never walked down the aisle with Tokee.

While I waited on Amon to get there, I rolled a blunt to take the edge off. I didn't know how this was going to play out, but I was ready for gunplay. No matter how mad I was at her, I would still bust a nigga's melon wide open 'bout that baby. I just needed a little time to myself. More than likely I would probably take a solo trip out of town for a while after I get her situated.

I put the blunt to my lips and took a pull, letting the smoke fill my lungs. The Kush had me feeling lov-a-lee, in my Plies voice. I sat back on plush leather and took a trip on Cloud 9.

Knock, knock!

The sound of the door had me on my feet like I was in the military. I took a look at my timepiece, and just like clockwork Amon showed up exactly twenty minutes later. I opened the door and we dapped each other up.

"What's up, my brotha?" Amon asked while making his entrance.

I closed the door behind him and went back to my favorite spot. Amon sat across from me. "I talked to Mercedes today, and she gave me an earful about your cousin."

"My cousin? She ain't 'wifey' no more?" he asked. I guess he was trying to see where my head was at.

"You know what I mean." I sat up with my elbows on my knees. "She with that nigga, Rich. Mercedes said he had her, too, but he let her leave as long as Barbee stayed to work off the debt with Giovanni."

Amon tilted his head to the side. "How the fuck is that gon' work? The nigga dead."

"Yeah, but she don't know that."

"So, in other words, he got her there on false pretenses?" Amon leaned forward and placed his hand underneath his chin.

"He has other plans for her. We gotta get my baby out of there, man."

"I'm 'bout that issue. Let's do it."

"Oh, yeah, the nigga's wife called and said she got info on Barbee. She said she saw her, so we gotta meet her now."

"Let's ride."

Rising up from my seat, Amon did the same. I grabbed the ratchet and we were out the door.

I-95N was moving pretty damn slow for non-working hours. Traffic wasn't bumper-to-bumper, but it was congested enough to get on my fuckin' nerves. "This that fuck-shit," I shouted while looking out the window at the trees we were passing slowly.

"Yeah, it is, but it ain't shit we can do about it." Amon kept his eyes on the road and his hand steady on the wheel.

"We should've took the back street or some shit."

"We gon' get there, bruh, just chill. I know this shit stressing you out, 'cause it's stressing me out, too. We gon' get her back."

"I know, man, the shit just fuckin' with me."

We spent thirty minutes slow-moving in traffic, and by the time we got to Yamato Road, we finally saw what the hold-up was about. A damn accident. It was a 4-car accident, and two of the lanes were blocked. We crept through for 10 more minutes until we passed it, and we were smooth sailing after that.

Amon had to be doing 100 on the dash, because we made it to Palm Beach Lakes Boulevard 15 minutes later. I called Michelle. She picked up on the third ring.

"Hello."

"I'm here."

"Come inside the garage, and you'll see me by the entrance to the store."

"Okay." I ended the call. "Go inside the garage. She's upstairs, waiting."

Amon drove up the ramp and parked next to her car. I rolled down my window so she could see me. Michelle eased out of the car with her big belly in tow. I didn't understand how married men cheated on their wives. Not only did it ruin the woman, but it damaged the kids. All that did was create trust issues with both parties in the future. Communication is the key when people not happy in their relationships. If a person's significant other won't change or fix the problem, then they should leave. There's no sense in dragging her along if he ain't happy. Shit, that's a waste of time. When I tied the knot, me and my wife were going to be forever. I didn't give a fuck if we had to sleep in separate rooms. *Ain't no divorce, bih!*

Michelle climbed into the backseat and closed the door. "Thank you so much for meeting me." She looked around like someone was watching her.

Me and Amon turned to face her. "Thanks for calling us," I said sincerely.

"I couldn't risk my husband catching y'all at the house."

"I feel you on that," I replied. "So, what info you got fo' me?" It was time to cut the small talk and get down to business.

"After I spoke with you, my mind went into overload. My husband had been out more than he had been in months. I always know when he's cheating because he spends less time at home and more time 'working.'"

"And what does that mean?" I was wondering what she was getting at.

"Let's just say we've been down that road before with his infidelities, and it could end badly for her. Anyway, today I followed him to his grandparents' house that he owns, and she was there. I kept looking at her to make sure I was certain, and I am."

I pulled my cellphone out and showed her the picture again. "This is who you saw earlier?"

Michelle took a good look at Barbee's picture. "Yes that's her," she nodded her head. "I'm positive."

"Where are they now?" Amon asked. He was ready to take Rich down just as much as me.

"At his grandparents' house. I'll give you the address."

Amon pulled out his cellphone. "What is it? I'll put it in my GPS."

Michelle passed him the address on a piece of paper. "Go now while they're still there and she's still breathing."

"A'ight, thanks." Amon said.

"You're welcome. I couldn't stand by and not say anything. He's been doing this for years, and I'm sick of it."

"I appreciate that," I replied.

When Michelle got out of the car and back into the safety of her own, we waited for her to back out before we followed the GPS to Rich's hideout. According to the directions, we were only 18 minutes away.

We went back out to Palm Beach Lakes Boulevard and hopped back on the interstate until we made it by the airport 14 minutes later. With less than four minutes away from our destination, the anticipation weighed in thick. I pulled out the ratchet to make sure it had one in the head, then I sat it on my lap and waited for us to pull onto Mozart Road.

Amon cruised the street slowly until we arrived at the house. There was a lot of land and a few bushes, so he parked next to the bush and kept the car running for a few. Night was just about to fall, so we waited a few extra minutes before getting out. I looked around to see if there were any neighbors, but I didn't see a single soul. I didn't see his car parked out front, either, but that didn't mean they weren't in there.

My cell started ringing. I looked at the screen and it was Mercedes calling, but I didn't answer.

"You ready?" Amon asked.

"Yeah."

Mercedes continued to call back-to-back, but she would have to wait. We stepped out of the car, dressed the same way we had done the first time around in our detective gear. "We knock on the door, and soon as he opens it, we running up in that bitch and laying his ass out."

"Cool." Amon replied. "Who keeps calling?"

"Mercedes. I'll call her back later."

We stepped onto the porch, my trigger finger started to itch as Amon knocked on the door and waited for an answer. My phone alerted me I had a text message, so I looked at it just in case she had something of importance to tell me.

Mercedes: I told Papa and Mama what happened and he had a heart attack. Please call me as soon as you can. We on our way to the hospital. I'm so scared.

"Fuck!" I shouted.

Chapter 15

Barbee

Out of all the places to go from Dade to Palm Beach County, Rich had us on the road heading to Jacksonville to Aqua Nightclub. Plies was performing the next night, and he was sure there would be plenty of ballers in the building. I rode shotgun with my arms folded underneath a blanket, looking at the stars up above.

"I don't understand why we going all the way up here for this when we could've stayed closer and got the same amount of cash, if not more."

"Niggas gon' pay to see Plies, and them check boys guaranteed to be in the building."

"Yeah, that's true, but it's different when you are at a strip club. You get to see who's spending the most money. Anybody can floss on a bottle, or even patch up, for that matter. In a strip club, broke niggas don't pay for dances. They're easier to distinguish amongst the rest."

"We needed to get away to a new area instead of making all the spots in our area hot. Besides, I can't risk being seen in my hometown. I know everybody."

"If you say so," I huffed. He was new to this shit. I been doing this, and he was randomly selecting a place for us to work based on assumptions. We had a fool-proof operation, and he was about to have us out here like two blind mice.

We had been on the road for a few hours, and we still had a few more to go. Corey was on my mind heavy, and I felt like I was committing the ultimate betrayal. Although everything that happened was against my will, the guilt was still present. I didn't have a choice, but to comply with Rich's demands. After listening to his wife, I realized I was in grave danger, and this

181

wasn't his first rodeo. I was just finding out I didn't know him at all. Good dick confused the best of us. *I know Rich got me!*

Me and Rich arrived in Jacksonville a little after midnight. We crashed at the Springhill Suites, which wasn't too far from the club. Inside the room there was a king size bed, and I knew he purposely did that. Shit, I would've been happy with two double beds. The room was nice, though it was rated at three stars. Since it was late, I opted out of taking a shower and slept fully clothed in the sweatpants I rode up in. I didn't need him rolling on me in the middle of the night, slipping his wood in me.

That ride had gotten the best of me. I wrapped myself up in the blanket tightly and closed my eyes.

I got up around noon. I guess I was really tired. Rich was watching television while smoking a blunt.

"Good morning, sleeping beauty."

Halfway asleep, I got up and stumbled toward the bathroom. "Hey," I said groggily.

Popping a squat over the toilet, I relieved myself of the urine that filled my bladder. I wasn't fond of hotel toilets, so I didn't want to rest my ass cheeks on their plastic seats, especially without my Clorox wipes. Wiping myself off, I flushed the toilet, then handled my daily hygiene before taking a quick shower.

For the majority of the time I stood underneath the warm water, I was collecting my thoughts. When I was done, I turned off the shower and slid open the glass door. I didn't bother drying off. I left myself wet intentionally and walked into the room where Rich was sitting. I stood in front of him and let the towel drop to the floor.

Rich's eyes expanded wide inside his head.

"Damn! Just like that, huh?"

"Yeah. I was thinking about what you said, and you're right." I inched toward him seductively with my finger in my mouth. His eyes were locked in.

"What's that?" he asked.

"That we need to be friends, since we are working together."

"Is that right?" Rich didn't blink once.

"Yes. I was upset, but then I remembered there was a time I had deep feelings for you. But then it all changed when I lost *our* baby. I couldn't face you, and then to find out you have kids hurt me more."

"I'm sorry, Barbee. I never knew about what Giovanni did. He never said a word. I love you, and I want to make another baby."

I lifted my leg and placed it on the chair where he was sitting and rubbed my clit. "But what about Michelle?"

"Fuck Michelle! I don't want her. I'll file for divorce as soon as we get back."

I slipped two fingers into my pussy and fingered myself. "Ah! You promise?" I moaned.

"I promise." Rich continued to watch me in amazement.

He had never seen me in action like this before. Removing both fingers from my juice box, I stuck them into my mouth and sucked my fingers.

"Damn, I like that freaky shit, bae."

I moved my fingers and played with my clit again. "You do?" I asked seductively.

"Hell yeah." I could hear the excitement in his voice.

"Well, lean forward and eat my pussy, just like this," I demanded.

Rich didn't hesitate with my demand. He dived tongue-first into my pussy and slurped away. The stubble from his mustache tickled my center as he ate away at the goodies.

"Mm, yeah. Just like that," I cried out with my eyes closed, pushing him further into my spot. "Suck that pussy, daddy."

Rich tried to suck my soul out of me, and I tried to keep myself mounted in the same position. The longer he feasted, the weaker my knees became. I could feel them buckle with every stroke of his tongue. After what seemed like forever, the sudden urge for me to pee presented itself.

"I'm about to cum," I purred like a kitten.

Rich lifted his head for a quick second. "Cum in my mouth," he instructed me, and of course I obliged.

"Ah!" I shouted as my orgasm took over my body and shook me like an earthquake. When Rich came up for air, his lips were extra wet. He held onto my waist, pushing me backward so he could get up. Without further notice, he pushed me toward the chair.

"Bend that ass over that chair."

I did as I was told and assumed the position. Looking back at him, he dropped his joggers and then his boxers before getting behind me. Rich slipped in, penetrating my pussy and stroking me deeply. I bit down on my lip and took every inch of him. See, he was a control freak, just like me, but in this position he knew he dominated me and could control how deep he went. I swear that shit felt like it was in my damn stomach, but it felt good at the same time.

"Stick your thumb in my ass," I moaned.

Rich did what he was told once again.

I didn't care what position we were in, I still needed to feel a sense of control. "Fuck me harder."

That round of sex lasted for twenty minutes, and he drilled me from the back the entire time. But hey, I wasn't complaining. After catching his nut, he carried me over to the bed and laid me down.

"I'm going to take a shower," Rich said, but not before giving me a sensual kiss on the lips.

"Okay." I replied.

I lay there for a few minutes until I heard the shower running. Leaping from the bed, I went over to his pants pocket to get his cellphone. Swiping the screen, I was disappointed to see he had a lock code on it. I tried to guess the code, but I couldn't get it right. The shower came to a sudden stop, so I put it back and got back into bed.

Rich stepped out with the towel wrapped around his waist. "You keep fuckin' me like that, and you can get a whole lot from me."

I laughed a little. "Is that a fact?"

"Yep, but you gotta leave that nigga alone." Rich walked over to where his pants were and took his cellphone out.

"Consider that done. I'm here with you, right? I haven't tried to escape. This is where I want to be, but you better leave Michelle and show me it's real."

"You ain't gotta worry about her. She know what it is."

"Oh, I'm not worried, and she better know." I extending my arms out to him. "Come on, and let's cuddle."

Rich dropped his towel and climbed into bed and underneath the covers with me, placing his cellphone on the nightstand. I placed a few kisses on his face and neck.

"Rich, I love you, too. I just don't know how to show it. Everything I've ever loved, I lost it."

He held me tight in his arms. "You won't lose me. Let's take a nap before we go out tonight, 'cause this gon' be a long one."

"Set your alarm."

Rich leaned back and grabbed his phone. I watched as he unlocked it, set the alarm, and put it back down. We were off to sleep in no time.

***

Plies had really brought the city out in Jacksonville. I swear everybody and they mammie was in the building. Big crowds were not my thing, but I had a job to do. The DJ had the club live, jamming Trick Daddy before Plies came on the stage. Everyone had cups in their left hands and their right hands in the air, rapping.

Anybody wanna muthafuckin' die come see I.

Who, me? T double-D, nigga

That's right, that's muhfuckin' me, nigga

And god damn it, if I said it, I muthafuckin' meant it

If it was fully, I muthafuckin' spit it, fuck whoever I offended

Hold on, wait one muthafuckin' minute!

The DJ let the beat drop from the beginning and started again. The crowd was hyped as they repeated the lyrics once again. The girl standing next to me was buck-wild.

"Girl, this is my jam," she shouted in my direction. Since I didn't know her, I didn't respond. She had been in the club for at least an hour, and she was lit like the Times Square Christmas tree. I knew this because she came in behind me and Rich.

Rich looked at me. "You know her?"

"Hell nah, she drunk as hell."

"Yeah, I know," he replied.

"I have to use the ladies' room. Come on," I shouted over the music.

"Okay, let's go."

Rich walked behind me closely, until we made it to the bathroom line. This was the one thing I hated about regular clubs: all the damn traffic!

186

"Go ahead. I'm going to stay right here until you come out." Rich posted up on the wall and watched the crowd.

"Okay, I'll be right out."

The lined moved at a snail's pace, and by the time I got inside, there was a line to use the toilet. In the corner by the sink there was a lady charging to use perfume, combs, brushes, hair spray, and lip gloss. One girl was tore up from the floor up, and she thought she looked good. But hey, if she didn't think so, who would? She had the nerve to have on this extra-small dress, exposing all three of her stomachs. Her thighs looked like ground beef, and her heels were crusty, like it was too much to get a pedicure.

The chick in front of me burst out in laughter and looked back at me. "I swear, some people don't care how they look when stepping out."

I thought it was funny, so of course I laughed, too. "I know, right? I was saying the same exact thing." I ain't never been a friendly-ass female, but she was a little tipsy, and there was no harm in a little bathroom humor while I waited.

A stall finally became available, and the girl in front of me stepped in. Two chicks walked in behind me, talking loud.

"Girl, I know damn well he not trying to act like he all that."

"Yeah, honey, he tried you big time. I know you not gon' let that slide? He all in VIP and shit, poppin' bottles and flashing his money."

The loudmouth chick had me at the word *money*, so my antennas extended to the max.

"Nah, girl. I know I better not see him talking to nobody or it's on. He ain't giving none of these bitches his money. You know he just came back from up top."

The funny girl came out and washed her hands. She walked past the two loud girls and bumped into one of them.

187

"Ex-scuuse you, damn."

"What?" she replied.

"You heard what I said." The loud girl rolled her eyes.

"No, baby, I don't speak Ebonics."

"Oh, I know your Bougie-ass didn't go there."

"Yes, I did. And it's *bourgeois*, so get it right, you bald-headed hood rat."

The ghetto girl threw her hands in the air. "So, what you wanna do?"

The perfume lady stood up. "Ain't no fighting in here. I'll call security, so keep it moving."

The ghetto girl's friend grabbed her arm. "Come on, girl, fuck this crazy shit."

The funny girl laughed. "Yeah, listen to your friend before I beatcha ass in here." With that being said, they turned and walked away.

By the time I used the restroom and was headed back to Rich, he was walking toward the door.

"You straight?" he asked with this mean mug on his face.

"Yeah, what's wrong?" I was hoping nothing happened while I was away.

"I heard two chick cappin' 'bout some chick they got into it with in the bathroom and thought it was you. So I came back here to see if I needed to beat a bitch's ass."

"Nah, they wasn't talking about me. They got into it with the chick that was standing in front of me."

"Oh, okay."

It was funny that he was ready to fight about me, but I had other shit on my mind, like this mystery nigga them hos was talking about in the bathroom. I grabbed his arm and pulled him down to my size. "The chicks was talking about some nigga that just came back from up top. He in the VIP section, so we need to get up there."

"Shit, let's go," Rich smiled.

We bumped our way through the crowd, and I swear the whole ordeal was getting on my fuckin' nerves. I hated it when people touch me, bump me, grab me, waste liquor on me, or burn me with ashes. I wasn't on that shit, so I maneuvered through the crowd gracefully, because I swear if anything happened from my list of don'ts, I would knock a bitch or nigga clean out. On my mama!

Rich was so focused on getting to the section that he wasn't looking back when I was grabbed.

I spun around on my heels quickly. "Get your fuckin' hands off of me!" When I looked up, the dude was laughing, but I recognized him right off the bat.

"Damn, girl, you still mean as fuck." Stoney smiled with a mouth full of golds.

"Shut up," I replied.

"Whatchu doin' up here?"

"Enjoying the nightlife."

Stoney chuckled a bit. "Still up to yo' old tricks, huh?"

"Nah. I stopped doing that."

"That's what's up. I ain't gon' hold you up. Good seeing you."

"You too."

Just as I was headed through the crowd, Rich was heading back in my direction. "What was you doing?" he asked.

"I lost you. You was walking so fast."

"Sorry about that. Come on." This time he grabbed my hand, keeping me close.

It had been a while since I last saw Stoney. Years, in fact. Stoney was Fox's nephew, and at the time I was running with him, Fox was teaching him the game. I was almost certain he was there for the same reason. The last thing I wanted to do was run into anybody I knew.

189

The VIP section was all the way live, and every female in the club was trying to get into that section. Locating this check-boy was easy as fuck, 'cause he was straight clowning and popping bottles. They bought out the bar and were taking pictures and going live on IG with tons of money. One of his homeboys glanced at the entrance, and there was a stampede of bitches begging to get in.

"Man, look at deez hos," the ringleader shouted.

"Them hos wanna ball with the IG stars," one of the misfits shouted to the bouncer. "Let them hos in. I'm trying to live like it's my last day."

Rich grinned. "I know that's right." He leaned in close to me and whispered in my ear. "Go sit close by so he can see you."

It was time to put the plan in motion. I added a little more swish in my hips and sashayed over to the balcony, and then to the couch to make sure he saw me. When we made eye contact, I made sure to flash a flirtatious smile. I sat down on the couch with my legs crossed and vibed to the music. Out of the corner of my eye, I watched him fix a drink and walk in my direction.

"Hey, beautiful. How you doing?"

I looked up and smiled. "I'm good, thank you."

"I'm Stefan. Can I offer you a drink?" He sat down beside me and held it out, but I didn't reach for it. "It's okay. I didn't do anything to it."

"You sure about that?" I asked.

"Positive." He kept his arm out. "You can come over and fix it yourself if you don't believe me."

"Okay, I'm taking you up on your word." I looked around. "If anything happens to me, all these people will know you did it." A slight giggle left my mouth.

"Trust me, I don't have a reason to do that."

"Okay, Stefan."

"Thank you. Um," he paused. "You haven't told me your name."

"That's because you didn't ask."

"My bad, beautiful. What's ya name and ya number?"

Stefan had a sense of humor, aside from him being so damn flamboyant. I could tell he was young. My guess was 22. Stefan was about 5'9" with brown skin. He wore his jewelry like Yo Gotti: multiple chains with a big Jesus piece.

"That's cute. I like that." I took a sip of my drink and looked him in his eyes. "My name is Jade." I leaned close to him, placed my hand on his thigh and whispered in his ear. "And if you keep me interested, I'll give you more than just my number after the club."

"Word," he laughed. "Shit, I like that idea."

They partied like animals for hours, and I partied just enough to seem drunk. The VIP section was over capacity, but that didn't stop the show, especially for Stefan, the ringleader and my soon-to-be victim. Stefan looked around for his friend and spotted him leaning over the balcony, throwing more money. He walked over to him and grabbed his arm. "Bruh, calm down before your ass fall."

"I'm showing deez niggas how to ball." He handed his cup to Stefan. "Fix me another drink."

Stefan walked back over to where I was sitting and fixed his boy a drink. "Don't you think he had enough?" I asked.

"This his last cup, 'cause he wasted." He poured a shot of Henny and sat the bottle down. "Beautiful, fix us another one."

"Okay."

When no one was looking I fixed us another drink and dropped a pill in Stefan's cup and stirred it up. Once it fully dissolved, I dropped an ice cube in it. Stefan walked back over and sat down.

"Here you go." I passed him the cup and he took a sip. "Thanks, beautiful."

"You're welcome." Then I sipped mine, as well.

The pill kicked in quickly, and Stefan began to feel woozy, so he sat his drink down and leaned back in the seat.

"Are you okay?" I asked.

"Yeah, I'm good."

"You sure?"

"Yeah." Stefan stood up, but lost his balance.

"Hold on, I got you." Jumping to my feet, I grabbed him by the waist and sat him back down. The last thing I needed was for his boys to get in the way of my money.

"I just need to sit here for a minute." His speech was slurred.

When I looked up, Rich was tapping his watch, signaling me to hurry up. "Come on, Stefan, I need to get you to your car."

"Hold up." Stefan leaned forward in a hurry and threw up in the ice bucket on the table. My reflexes allowed me to move back, because I didn't know where he was dropping his fluids. He sat there hunched over for a few minutes before lifting his head.

"You okay?"

"Yeah. Let's go, unless I done embarrassed myself."

"Nah, you good."

Stefan got up and hollered at his boys, and I followed behind him. There were three of them total. "Y'all boys, come on."

They stopped what they were doing and followed us out of the VIP section. "They going with us?" I asked.

"Yeah, we rode together. We staying at the same hotel."

"I don't get down like that."

"We not in the same room. Calm down, beautiful. What type of nigga you think I am? I don't share."

Stefan had me thrown for a moment. I was ready to call the whole thing off if they were sharing rooms.

Chapter 16

Barbee

After we left the club, Stefan drove to the Hampton Inn. The damn hotel was literally up the street from ours, and it made me feel uncomfortable. After tonight we needed to get ghost in the early morning, because it was just too close in distance. Stefan was still tipsy, but he wasn't as wasted as he should've been thanks to his body rejecting the pill.

Stefan parked the truck and we all got out. Clicking the locks, he turned on the alarm and walked close to me so he could hold my hand. I put the purse I was carrying on the opposite side and clutched it tight.

"You nervous?" He intertwined his fingers with mine.

"Should I be?"

"Nah, I won't do nothing you won't allow me to."

"Aren't you a gentlemen?"

"I'd like to think so."

"Somebody raised you right."

"Yeah, my granny."

We walked through the lobby, and I was trying my best to keep my head down and avoid all cameras, so I played drunk and leaned on Stefan's shoulder. From my peripheral vision, I could peep the hood chick watching us walk through. That bitch was probably thinking they 'bout to run a train on me.

All of us took the elevator to the fourth floor, and my heart started to beat faster than normal. I told myself they were in different rooms, but the same floor. We stopped at room 408 and everyone else kept walking, so I felt a little relieved.

Stefan opened the door and let me in, but he stood at the door, talking to one of his boys. I slipped into the bathroom and shot Rich a quick text of the room number.

When I came out, Stefan was still at the door talking, so I sat my purse on the side of the bed out of plain sight. Five minutes passed and he was still there, and if I knew anything about Rich, he was coming up 10 minutes later. He didn't believe in leaving me in the room for longer than a 15-minute time period.

If I didn't think fast we would be busted soon, so I did what I had to do to get his attention. I stripped out of my dress, wearing a black lace thong with the matching bra, and strutted to the door, displaying each and every chocolate curve on my body. Stefan felt my presence and turned around.

"Damn!" Stefan's mouth dropped. I was certain he had never been with a beautiful, dark-skinned goddess. Stefan turned back to whomever he was talking to in the hallway and dismissed him. "I'll holla atchu later." He closed the door and turned to face me. "You got my attention."

"Good."

Stefan walked up to me and grabbed a handful of my ass. "That ass soft. I wanna see that shit jiggle while I hit it from the back."

He kissed me on my neck. Our bodies had become connected while we took several steps toward the bed. I stopped when I felt the heel of my foot touch the bedframe.

Placing me on the bed gently, he climbed on top of me and kissed my succulent breasts. What I needed him to do was go into the bathroom and brush his damn teeth.

"Don't you wanna shower first?"

"Nah, I'm good."

"Well, I want you to. Brush ya' mouth while you at it." I giggled, but I was dead-ass serious. Throw-up and alcohol was not a good smell.

"Only if you come with me."

Fuck! I was screwed. "Okay."

We walked into the bathroom and he turned on the shower. Then he undressed himself placing his clothes and jewelry on the sink. His ass made sure he grabbed his toothbrush and toothpaste. I removed my bra and panties and sat them next to his clothes. I waited until he stepped into the shower to walk out, grab the key, and slip it under the door for Rich.

When I hit the door, Stefan was coming out of the bathroom. "Whatchu doing?"

"Nothing. I thought I heard my phone ring."

Stefan was acting strange. We went into the shower and took a bird bath. I was praying that Rich would make it in the nick of time because I didn't like the way this was going. Felt like I was losing control because he wasn't faded enough.

After we were done, we walked into the room, but there was no Rich. *Shit!* My body shook like I had a mild touch of Parkinson's disease. Stefan walked up to me, pushed me on the bed, and climbed on top of me, kissing me again, but more aggressive.

"You ready to get this party started?"

"I thought that's what we were doing?"

"Nah, we missing something."

"Like what?"

Stefan stood up, walked to the adjoining door, and unlocked it. His homeboy walked in, smiling wide as fuck, showing all 32 and his goddamn tonsils. Nigga just knew his dick was about to dip into something hot, wet, and creamy. But he had me all the way fucked up. In just a minute I was about to turn that smile upside down.

"Choo-choo," he sang, bouncing his shoulders up and down.

"Stefan, what are you doing?" I sat up on the bed and scooted toward the headboard.

197

"It ain't no fun if the homie can't have none." Stefan laughed before he closed the door and locked it.

Where the fuck is Rich? Did he set me up?

Stefan's homeboy unbuckled his pants and let them fall to the floor. "She fine, too, bruh." Stefan slapped hands with his boy. "We gon' fuck the air outta this one. The fine ones always hos, my boy!" he added.

"Who you telling?" Stefan added.

"I'm down with a train," I replied. "Just let me get some protection."

"Ooh, bruh, she strapped and ready for the dick." They laughed.

I reached down on the side of the bed and dug my hand inside of my purse. Out came a 380-caliber handgun, locked and loaded. Both of these niggas had me fucked up.

I aimed it at them and used my left hand to place the silencer on the tip.

"What the fuck you doin'?" Stefan asked.

"This my protection. You didn't think I was pulling out condoms, did you?" It was my turn to laugh.

"Put the gun down, shawdy. You don't wanna do this," Stefan pleaded. His homeboy didn't say shit.

"Shut the fuck up and sit on the floor." I got up from the bed. "Oh, shit ain't funny no mo', huh?"

A noise from the side of me caught my attention and I jumped, aiming my shit toward the noise.

Rich jumped and put his hand out. "Chill, bae, it's me."

"What the fuck took you so long?"

"What the fuck you doing naked?" he barked. This nigga was crazy as a road lizard, doing all this yelling.

"I didn't have a choice since it took you so long, and lower your fuckin' voice."

"I wanted to see how you handled business and to make sure no one else was coming in." Rich walked over to me and aimed his Glock .40 at both of those cowards. "Get dressed, and hurry yo' ass up. Showing my pussy and shit. Fuck wrong with you?"

I ignored him and went into the bathroom and got dressed. On the way out I took all of Stefan's jewelry and put it in the bag Rich brought up.

"Put on those gloves in that bag and wipe down everything you touched and clean house."

I went through his luggage and found a small handbag full of money. I tossed that in the bag, too.

"Go check the other room and take this nigga's shit, too."

Grabbing my pistol, I unlocked the door and went into the other room slowly, making sure no one else was in there. I went through all of his shit and found a shoebox full of money and plenty of jewelry.

I walked in with a huge grin on my face. "These niggas loaded. Somebody did say y'all just came from up top."

With my gun in hand, I walked over to Stefan's homie and smacked him across the head with the gun.

"Argh!" he shouted, holding his head. Blood was running down his arm.

"And watch yo' mouth, pussy-ass nigga. I ain't no ho, but I rob hos like you, though."

Stefan knew what time it was. He started to ease back in the corner, as if that was going to stop what was about to happen to him. "It ain't no fun if the homie can't have none, huh?"

He didn't reply.

"What's wrong? The cat got your tongue?" I asked. Leaning down in front of him, I tapped him on the lips with the barrel. "Open your mouth, 'cause this my homie, and he want some, too."

When he didn't reply, I hit him upside the head too, drawing blood. Stefan was trying to remain cool and not scream. "Open your mouth right muthafuckin' now," I spoke through gritted teeth. Stefan realized I wasn't no joke and did what I said. I slid my gun in his mouth. "I outta make you suck the bullets out my pistol, you fuck-ass nigga. You a ho, ya mama a ho, ya grand mammie a ho, and if you got daughters, they gon' be hos, too." They had me heated, so I had to let it be known I didn't fuck off.

"Let's go before his entourage come down here, too," Rich said, reminding me we didn't have more time to waste.

Stefan just sat there, looking at me in utter shock. I slid the gun slowly in and out of his mouth like it was a dick. "Don't ever try a bitch like me. I'll make you commit suicide."

Snatching my gun from his mouth, I chipped his tooth in the process. Ask me if I cared? *Fuck no!*

Rich was standing there with his gun still aimed and ready to fire. I walked past him. "Come on, bae, let's go."

We backed up out of the room and crept out slowly, down the hallway and to the stairwell, hoping their doors were like Comfort Inn and Suites to avoid the cameras once again.

The next day I was up early. The way last night played out wasn't sitting too well with me. I had never run into an issue like that, and it could've ended badly. All I wanted to do was get back to my neck of the woods. As I watched Rich sleep, he reminded me of a gentle, psycho giant with a mean streak. I never knew who I was dealing with, especially if he didn't take his medicine.

A few minutes later Rich finally rolled over, and that was what I was waiting on. I put my face close to his and played with his eyelids. "Wake up."

"I'm tired. What time is it?" Rich yawned, blowing his hot breath in my face. I was sure he burned off my eyebrows.

"10:23," I said, looking over at the bright alarm clock.

"It's still early. Come lay with me."

"Rich, I don't feel comfortable here. We should leave. My gut is telling me something is about to happen, and it never steers me wrong."

Rich stroked the side of my face gently, like I was delicate flower he was afraid to ruin. "Barbee, I would never let anything happen to you. If any one of them niggas would've touched you, I swear I would've made they shit look like ground beef."

Rich kissed me softly with his morning breath, and I reciprocated. Our tongues did the slow wind, and that was enough to get my juices flowing. Rich's hands explored my body as he searched for the hidden treasure. A tingling sensation shot up my spine when his fingers fondled my clitoris. Closing my eyes, I allowed nature and Rich to take its course. My body was here with Rich, but my mind was elsewhere.

Several hours later, we finally got up. We had slept the entire day away. The sun had left its footprints across the sky, and the stars were making their grand appearance. We both stretched and yawned on one accord, like it was rehearsed.

"I was thinking we could hit one more lick before we take it back home. Besides, we still have one more day here."

Rich must have dreamed long and hard about it, but he could keep on dreaming, 'cause it wasn't gon' happen. "Things happen when you get greedy. We took over $50K from them niggas, and that's a damn good lick, considering the circumstances."

"Come on, bae, just one more."

"Rich, baby, listen to me, please. My mind never steers me wrong. Just like last night, I knew some foul shit was about to go down before it even happened." I kissed his face. "Just listen to me for once, please."

Rich sat and thought for a moment before he opened his mouth. "A'ight, pack it up and let's get outta here."

"Thank you, baby." I jumped up happily and packed my shit, 'cause I was ready to get the fuck outta dodge.

Thirty minutes later we were all packed up and ready to go. The money we had taken was placed in my suitcase. Rich tossed the key cards on the dresser, walked to the door, and opened it. I rolled my suitcase out and headed toward the elevator. Rich was behind me, making sure everything was Gucci.

We stepped out into the night air, and I hightailed it to the car. It wasn't cold, but it was cool, to say the least. My purse was on my side, and my hand was resting peacefully on that piece of steel. If anything was to pop off, I was ready to dump these slugs in somebody's child, father, or brother.

Rich unlocked my door and put our bags in the trunk of his car. Sitting in the front seat took some of the edge off, and I was finally able to breathe freely. All of it wouldn't be gone until we were on the highway on our way home.

As soon as I closed my eyes, the sound of fireworks stopped my heart. I jumped from my seat to see where it was coming from, but I couldn't see. Then I heard something ricochet off the window, so I ducked down in the seat.

"Rich!" I screamed. "Where are you?" The sound of gunshots came from the side of the car.

"Baby, cut the car on."

There was no need to respond due to my survival tactics kicking in. Ain't no telling what I would do since my life was in danger. I put the key in the ignition and cranked that bitch up. "Let's go," I screamed, but it fell on deaf ears, and the gunshots never stopped.

Destiny Skai

Chapter 17

Barbee

My heart was pounding out of my chest. I knew some shit was about to go down. Rich jumped in the car, closed the door, and burned rubber pulling out. We flew out into oncoming traffic without looking, and by the grace of God we both were unharmed. I remained silent until we got onto I-95.

"What the fuck happened back there?" I was pretty much winded from all that yelling.

"Niggas from the hotel last night just recognized me and started blasting." Rich was sweating profusely. I opened the glove box to look for napkins. Leaning over in the seat, I wiped his face and examined his body closely.

"I thought you were hit." I was relieved we got away unharmed.

"Nah, I saw the nigga, but I played it cool and he upped the strap and missed. I shot his ass, though."

"I heard something hit the window, and that's when I ducked."

Rich glanced at me. "Bulletproof windows. When you work for someone like Giovanni, you never know who watching or trying to murk you. I told you I wouldn't let anything happen to you, but you still don't trust me."

I exhaled slowly. "Can you blame me? I mean, you kidnapped me, did and said all type of crazy shit to me to keep me around. What do you expect from me? I know you won't let anyone else hurt me, but I believe you will hurt me."

"I won't hurt you. I love you too much for that, and to prove it to you, I'm going to delete that out my phone."

"You have a funny way of showing it," I pouted, but I was happy to hear that. I watched him as he pulled his phone out and delete the footage that haunted me.

"I'm gon' be honest with you." He paused and continued to watch the road.

"What is it?"

"I have a condition that makes me spazz out and do things I wouldn't do if I take my meds on a regular basis." My ears were at attention. "I have a personality disorder, and I've been like this for years. Since I was a teenager."

"That explains your mood swings and temper." I knew about his condition, but now he was opening up to me about it.

"Yes, and rejection is my weak point. That will turn me into a monster, and after that I'm uncontrollable. All I want is to be with you. I don't care about you robbing Giovanni or what you do, 'cause we can be on some Bonnie and Clyde shit. I mean, that's only if you want to continue with your hustle."

For the next few hours Rich and I discussed his childhood. That made me feel a lot of sympathy for him, and I finally understood him as a person. That didn't justify his actions, but it opened my eyes to what he went through. Rich blamed his mother for calling the police on him and having him Baker Acted because the time he spent in the facility only made him worse. I sat back and got comfortable with my blanket and listened to him talk.

During some portion of the ride I fell asleep, because when I woke up I saw Palm Beach signs. I sat up in my seat. "Damn we made it back fast," I said in between yawns.

"Yeah, you were knocked out, but I had my music to keep me company since my sidekick was outta there." Rich got off on our exit. "You hungry?"

I looked at the time on the dash. It was after two in the morning. "Nah, I don't eat this late."

206

"Watching ya weight, huh?"

"Something like that."

"Okay, well, we can go to breakfast in the morning, then."

"Cracker Barrel?"

"Sounds good to me."

It only took us ten minutes to get to the house. The neighborhood was dark and quiet. We were the only movement that could be seen at that time of morning. I observed my surroundings and took notes on what was around me. This was a good duck-off spot, and I could see why he brought me here from the beginning.

Rich shook his keys to grab my attention. "Go open the door and I'll bring in the bags."

"Okay."

My legs were cramped from the long ride, so I stretched them out before taking the walk up to the porch. I unlocked the door and left it open for Rich while I went to the bathroom. I had been holding my pee for a minute now.

In the bedroom, I placed my purse underneath the bed and took giant steps to the toilet. Nervousness took over my body as I sat in deep thought. Tonight could've been my last night on earth if he didn't have those bulletproof windows.

Rich stood in the door of the bathroom, watching me. "You okay?"

"Yeah."

"You sure?"

"Yeah, I'm good. I promise."

"Are you having any regrets about us?"

"No. This is where I want to be, and I'll show you when I get up."

Rich leaned against the door, grinning and folding his arms. "That was some gangsta-ass shit you did at the hotel. That shit made a nigga's dick rock up. If them niggas wasn't so deep in that bitch, I would've fucked you right there in the room and show them how I beat the pussy they wanted."

Rich was fascinated with the way I handled business and maintained myself as a classy woman. I was a lady goonette in his eyes. There wasn't a bitch breathing that could wear my stilettos.

Rich watched me closely as I wiped myself and washed my hands. We were two feet apart, so I reached out and grabbed his dick.

"I got you hard right now."

"Always."

"Let's take this in there." Nodding my head toward the room, I grabbed his hand and led the way. "Take off your clothes."

When I had him fully naked, I pushed him on the bed. "I like that aggressive shit, but I want you to sit all that ass and pussy on my face."

I rubbed my clit, soaking my finger with its juices, and shoved it in his mouth. "In due time, baby. Right now I wanna please you." I stroked his dick with my left hand. "I'm about to suck the skin off your dick," I moaned.

"Damn, I love yo' ass."

"I love you, too."

Rich closed his eyes when he felt me spit on his dick and jack that muthafucka slowly. Using my right hand, I eased my hand underneath the bed and grabbed the gun. I rose to my feet and rubbed his inner thigh with it.

"How does that feel?" I asked him.

"Cold as fuck." Rich opened his eyes. "Bae, what the fuck you doing?"

"Putting an end to all the bullshit you put me through."
Pow!

Rich screamed and grabbed his thigh. "Argh!" Blood squirted from his wound and onto the bed. He rocked back and forth. "Bitch, I'ma kill you!"

"Not before I kill you."

I aimed the gun at his chest and prepared to squeeze the trigger, but before I could get the round off he grabbed my hand and threw my arm to the side, making a hole in the wall. I punched him where the hole was in his leg, and he screamed out in excruciating pain. Rich was strong because he never let go of my hand. He used every muscle in his body to squeeze my hand. After a while it became numb, and I let the gun go, causing it to crash on the floor, setting off another round.

Rich leapt from the bed and grabbed me, knocking me to the floor. I winced in pain as my back hit the floor with a loud thump. He climbed on top of me and punched me in my face and mouth. Blood leaked from my mouth and down my throat. Rich rose up and tried to hit me again, but I moved to the side and his fist hit the floor. I knew that shit hurt 'cause he tumbled, allowing me space to get loose.

Once I was on my feet, I picked the gun up off the floor and ran toward the door. In the process, Rich stuck his foot out and tripped me. I crashed headfirst into the hallway. I could only vaguely see him coming toward me thanks to the blood in my eye. I aimed and pulled the trigger in his direction. Then he disappeared. I didn't know if I hit him or not, but I wasn't about to sit around and find out.

Stumbling down the hallway and bumping into everything in sight, I made it to the front door. As soon as I opened the door, I ran down the steps as fast as my feet would allow me. The blood from my eye was pouring out like tears, and it made it difficult to see, but that didn't stop me.

The grass was wet as I ran through it. I looked back toward the door to make sure Rich wasn't following me. When I turned around, I bumped into a male figure. I was praying it wasn't his cousin.

"Please help me! He's trying to kill me."

The stranger grabbed me by my arms and took the gun from my palm.

"Please don't hurt me," I cried.

I felt him scoop me up and place me over his shoulders and walk me toward the road. I could see one street light shining, and that was it. I heard a car door open, and he sat me in the backseat.

"What the fuck happened to her?" the driver asked.

I rubbed my eyes with my shirt to get the blood out and to see who the familiar voice belonged to. My vision wasn't the greatest, but my ears were just fine. Blinking a few times, I squinted my eyes to catch focus on the shadow in front of me. I knew my eyes were playing tricks on me, and it was too good to be true.

"Amon?"

"Yeah, baby, it's me."

I looked to my right. "Corey?"

"Yeah, it's me."

"I thought I would never see you again."

Corey wrapped his arms around and held me tight. "Me too, baby. Me too." Corey rubbed my back. "Who all in the house?"

"Only Rich."

"Okay, stay in here, and we'll be right back."

Before he could close the door, I stopped him. "Be careful. He has a gun. And there's a pink suitcase at the door; grab that, please."

"We'll be right back." He closed the door, but he didn't walk away just yet. No matter what, I felt safe seeing the both of them.

***

Corey

Seeing Barbee like that really fucked me up. Me and Amon had been sitting in the cut for a couple of hours, waiting on them to show up. It wasn't until 2:00 a.m. that we saw some headlights hit the street. We sat back and watched Barbee and this nigga get out of the car. When she got out of the car, she was smiling and shit. That hurt a nigga's heart. Then she went and opened the door while he brought in their luggage. Apparently they had just got back in town.

I told Amon we needed to wait and allow them to get comfortable before we bum-rushed that shit. Ten minutes had passed, and I heard a noise that sounded like a gunshot, but Amon said he didn't hear anything, so we stayed put. It wasn't until the last shot that I got out of the car and headed toward the house, just to be on the safe side.

When I was halfway to the house, I saw Barbee run out of the door, and that's when I intercepted her. Seeing her bruised and battered face broke me down, 'cause now I didn't know what to believe.

"Come on, bruh, we ain't got all day." Amon tapped me on the shoulder.

"I'm ready."

Me and Amon ran to the house and through the front door. The first thing I saw was the suitcase she told me to get. My ratchet was in my hand as I made my way down the hallway. Amon was behind me, covering my back. The light shining brightly took me the room where I assumed they slept at, but I didn't see anyone.

"I'll check the other room." Amon walked away, and I looked around the room. On the floor I saw a purse. I picked it up, realizing it belonged to Barbee. Just seeing that she had things here made me question what was really going on in here.

I took a few steps toward the bathroom, and when I peeked in Rich hit my hand, but my grip was so tight on the gun I didn't drop it. Bringing my arm forward, I hit him in the face with it. Rich tussled with me, trying to take the gun, but I was stronger than him. I pushed him against the sink, hitting him repeatedly over the head with the ratchet. His body went limp as he lost consciousness, causing him to lean on me. Placing my gun to his stomach, I fired one shot and pushed him into the tub.

Amon came in at the last minute. "You killed the nigga?"

"Where the fuck were you?"

"In the basement, checking shit out. And Mercedes wasn't lying. This nigga got ropes and chairs in that bitch."

"A'ight, let's clear it."

On the way out, I grabbed Barbee's purse and her luggage and fled the crime scene.

Chapter 18

Barbee

A stinging sensation hit my eye. I tried desperately to stop it by rolling onto my side. When I cracked my eyes open just a little, I realized it was the sun blinding me. The stabbing pain in my head was unbearable. Raising my hand to my face, I felt something pointy and extreme puffiness around the socket. It was like my eye had come out of the socket. I panicked as shock took me over. I looked around the room in absolute terror. Rich had me shook, and that god-awful dream didn't make it no better.

A nurse walked in wearing glasses. "You're awake," she smiled.

"Yes, and I have a terrible headache." I rubbed my temple. "And my body feels like I was hit by a semi-truck."

"On a scale of one to ten, how would you describe the pain?" she asked.

"Forty," I answered.

She laughed. "Okay. I'll get you something for the pain." The nurse walked away, but she stopped and turned back to face me. "The gentlemen that came here with you, they're down the hall visiting someone else, but I'll tell them you're awake. They also spoke with the police, but I'm not sure what was said. All I know is they left their card for you to give them a call and file a police report."

Two minutes after the nurse left, the door opened and in walked Corey. "How you feeling?" Corey walked over and sat down on the bed beside me.

"It feels like someone is stabbing me in the face, but other than that I'm okay."

"That's good to hear." Corey broke our eye contact and looked down at the floor. He didn't have to say anything because I knew he had so many questions for me. I also knew he was hurting. I could see it in his eyes and his body language.

"Corey, what's wrong?" I rubbed his hand, but he was silent, and that wasn't like him. "Please talk to me."

"Nothing. I'm okay."

"I know you, and you not telling the truth."

"We'll talk later. Just focus on getting better. That's my only concern: to make sure you get out of here."

"Corey, I hope nothing has changed between us. I love you, and I thought about you every day."

"I loved you, too, and I did the same."

"Wait! You said *loved*. That's past tense, Corey. What are you saying?"

"I still love you. That hasn't changed." There was a pregnant pause. "Amon is going to take care of you and keep you safe until I get back. I changed the locks on the door and installed an alarm. He has the key and code for you."

That made me sit up and tilt his head toward me. His eyes were turning red and full of tears. "Corey, what's wrong? Where are you going?"

"I'm going away for a while, but I'll be back." The tears started to fall and stream down his cheeks. He wiped them away with the back of his hand.

"Why?"

"There's so much going on in my head, and I need time to think things through."

"Corey, don't do this, please."

"Barbee, please give me time to myself right now."

"What about the wedding?"

"That's not gon' happen."

214

My own tears started to fall, rolling down my cheeks along with his. The teardrops burned my eyes as they traveled south.

Corey pulled his hand from my grip and stood up. "I have to go. I can't do this."

"Don't leave me, please!" Corey walked away, ignoring my cries. "Corey!" I screamed to the top of my lungs. My heart shattered into a million pieces when he didn't look back.

***

The next day I was discharged from the hospital, but before I left I stopped by my father's room to visit him. See, after Corey left me, Amon showed up and told me my father had a heart attack when he heard about the kidnapping, but he was doing better.

I also asked him questions about Corey, but he wouldn't tell me anything. I was lost and hurt at the same time because I didn't understand how he could leave me at a time like this, when I needed him the most. Everything I'd been through the entire time I was with Rich doesn't compare to the pain I felt when Corey walked out of that hospital room and out of my life.

On my way home (I wasn't even sure if that was the appropriate name for it anymore since Corey wasn't there) I cried myself to sleep in the backseat of Amon's car. I felt a gentle push on my arm, and when I opened my eyes, it was Mercedes.

"Wake up. You're home."

She and Amon helped me out of the car. My body was in so much pain after fighting Rich and falling on the floor. We took baby steps all the way to the front door.

Amon unlocked the door and let us in. The alarm was beeping, so he silenced it. "Come on so we can put you in bed and you can get some rest."

"Okay."

The walk down the hallway seemed long, and I caught flashbacks of Rich and me fighting in here before he took me from my happy place.

They placed me on the bed and pulled the covers over my weak, sore body. "Thank you."

"No need for that. That's what family is for," Amon replied.

"That's right." Mercedes kissed me on my cheek. "We're not going anywhere. We'll be right out in the living room if you need us."

"Where is Sierra? Did she leave with Corey?" I hadn't seen her since I returned, not even in the hospital.

"No, she's with Dre." Amon knew more questions were coming, so he stopped me when my lips moved. "Don't ask. You'll find out everything in due time. Just get some rest, B." Amon closed the door when Mercedes walked past him, leaving me alone with a million questions in my head and no answers.

It was painful to move around, but I needed to find my cellphone. I leaned over to the nightstand, and the first thing I noticed was a manila envelope with my name on it, big as day in Corey's handwriting.

With my fingers trembling, I picked up the envelope and sat it on my lap. I didn't know what to expect when I opened it. I peeked inside and saw a lot of paper, so I pulled it out slowly. On top was a sticky note:

I hope this package helps you understand my reasons for leaving you at a time like this.

The images on the paper increased my breathing, and I could feel myself hyperventilating. My body trembled with fear. In my hands were copies of text messages and phone calls between me and Rich. And yes, they were stamped with the date and time. The papers slipped from my fingertips, and I cried like a newborn baby.

At that moment I knew I had lost Corey forever.

***

Rich

I woke up to the beeping sound of the heart monitor at St. Mary's Medical Center, all because Barbee was a liar. When I got out of the hospital, I was going to pay her ass a visit.

I sat up in the bed and pulled the IV out of my arm. It stung a little, but I was a G. I knew the nurses would be back within the hour, so I moved as quickly as I could. Snatching off the gown, I put on the scrubs I stole from the closet. From the window I could see it would be dark soon, and I needed to move fast.

I picked up the bag on the chair. Inside were two cell-phones, but one of them wasn't mine, and my car keys. I walked over to the door and cracked it open just a little. The nurse's station was empty, so I made a go for it. I wasn't in the best condition, but I had to force my body to move a little quicker than it was. Stopping by the wall, I peeked and made sure no one was there before I slipped by. I was a few feet from the elevator door, so I pushed myself harder. Pressing the elevator button, I waited impatiently for it to come up from the first floor. I was nervous as fuck. As soon as the doors opened, I was greeted by the food service chick who was bringing up my dinner. I dropped my head and stepped into the elevator so she wouldn't notice me as she stepped out.

"Hey, where are you going?" she asked, looking at the scrubs I was wearing. "You haven't been discharged yet, and it's my duty to let them know you're leaving."

"Mind yo' fuckin' business, bitch." I pressed the button to close the doors on that funky ho and got out of dodge.

Five minutes later I was in the parking lot. According to the nurse, I somehow drove myself to the hospital. I found it funny Michelle hadn't been to see me. I clicked the panic button on my key ring for the next ten minutes before I finally heard my car. After all that walking, I just knew my ass was gon' pass out at any minute.

Once I was safely inside the car I pulled out the burner phone and checked the call log. My eyes stretched to the max when I saw a number I recognized. Now, my next question was what the fuck her number was doing in this nigga's phone? I called that bitch from the number to find out.

"Thank you for returning my call. I've been waiting to see if you found them at the address I gave you." She hesitated. "Is he dead?"

"Nah, bitch, I ain't dead, but you about to be."

"Rich?" Michelle asked.

"Yeah, bitch, my heart still ticking."

Michelle hung up the phone, so I knew she was about to leave the house. My engine roared when I turned the key over, and I hauled ass out of the parking lot, trying to catch her before she fled with the kids. This bitch was gon' die today. Michelle betrayed me and set me up. Now it all made sense as to how this nigga was able to find Barbee.

A sharp pain zipped through my body, and my vision seemed blurry. Images of last night's events played through my head like a movie.

I woke up in the bathtub with gunshot wounds in my stomach and thigh. I was in so much pain I could hardly move. Somehow I found the strength to pull myself from the tub and onto the floor. My body crashed onto the cold, hard, tiled floor. The constant flow of blood that left my body made me realize death was around the corner.

As I slithered across the floor like a spineless snake, I stumbled across what appeared to be a burner phone. The nigga dropped it during our little tussle. Clutching it tightly in my hand, I continued to crawl on my elbows until I made it into the bedroom.

It was a struggle, putting on my clothes, but if I didn't do it I was sure to die. I gritted my teeth as I pulled up my boxers and jeans. Placing my hand over the hole in my stomach, I tried to stop the blood. That shit didn't work. After sitting for a few minutes, I was able to pull a t-shirt over my head. There was no way I would make it crawling around on the floor, so I stood on my feet and held onto the wall with my gun in my hand.

Fifteen minutes later I was out the door and limping to my car. Before I got in I tossed the gun in the bushes, just in case the police showed up at this address. Once inside the car, I reached into the backseat and grabbed my jacket and put it on. After that I drove myself to the hospital, halfway conscious. Calling the ambulance would've been much easier, but I didn't need the police in my shit, turning it into a crime scene.

Just the thought of last night turned me into a mad man, and now this shit with Michelle. My blood was boiling, and I could feel the steam coming from my ears. I punched the steering wheel.

"I swear to God on my kids, I'm killing this bitch," I shouted.

My foot was pressed down hard on the accelerator, and my Dodge Challenger was flying through traffic like I was in a muthafuckin' jet. All I wanted to do was get to my soon-to-be-ex wife and strangle her to death. I didn't give a fuck that my kids weren't gon' have a mother. Shit, I'd find them a new one.

Out of nowhere my head started to spin, leaving me light-headed and seeing doubles. I couldn't tell if I was coming or going. The car in front of me slammed on its brakes, and I did the same, but I couldn't stop fast enough.

Trying to avoid a rear-end accident, I turned the wheel hard and veered off onto the sidewalk. The light post was coming toward me fast, and I tried to stop, but I was no longer in control. My car flew head-on into the post, and my whole body jerked, crashing into the steering wheel.

Beeeeep!

The extended sound of the horn was the last thing I heard before I closed my eyes.

Chapter 19

Barbee

One month later

Tonight was the grand opening for Chyna's Dolls. Me and Mercedes were beyond excited. We dedicated so much time into making everything perfect, and that was the way I expected my night to go. Things hadn't been that smooth during my transition, but I was making it. I had to learn to take it one day at a time.

Corey and I were not together. In fact, I hadn't heard from him since that day at the hospital, but Sierra spoke to him quite often. She said he asked about me, but that was it. It was hard living without him, but there was nothing I could do about it. Maybe he would find it in his heart to forgive me, and maybe he wouldn't. I knew what type of man I was dealing with, but at the time I was more into getting money at any cost. It just so happened that this mind frame cost me the thing I loved the most. In the life I led, I didn't care about a man, but Corey said he would change me completely. And he did. He turned me into a lover, and now I was brokenhearted all over again.

Word on the street was Corey left Florida altogether and would not disclose his location. Sierra didn't know where he went. Neither did Amon, and that was his best friend. In due time, I knew he would reappear because I was still living in his place with Sierra. The bills were still being paid by him. I tried to locate him through a trace, but we couldn't find where the payments came from. All I wanted to do was find him and plead my case. That wasn't happening, though. He made sure of that.

Standing at the mirror, I gave myself a look-over, and I was happy with the woman I was looking at. I had come a long way from the old me, and I promised myself I was going to enjoy the opening while running my business at the same time. As much as I loved Corey, I couldn't stop living my life. A month ago I could've been dead, but my life was spared. As promised, I told myself if he ever came back, I would do any- and every-thing in my power to get him back and make him feel secure about marrying me. There was no one I could see myself with besides him.

A lone tear slipped from my eye, streaking my makeup. Quickly I grabbed a piece of tissue and tapped it softly to keep it from smearing. "Stop it, Barbee," I whispered to myself.

It was time to head up to the club and end my pity party. On my way out I peeked in at Sierra. She was lying on her side, Facetiming who I assumed to be Dre, judging by the huge smile on her face. Whatever he was saying, she was eating it up, because I could barely see her irises.

"Hey, boo, I'm goin' to the club."

Sierra's eyes lit up with excitement. "Barbee, you look gorgeous! If only Corey—" She paused. "I'm sorry."

"It's okay. No more tears, right?"

"No more tears," she smiled. "Have fun."

"I will. Goodnight."

"Goodnight."

I closed the door and walked away. Mercedes was waiting on me in the living room.

"Ready?"

"As ready as I'm gon' be." I turned around in a full circle, showing off my strapless one-piece, all-white pantsuit that hugged all of my voluptuous curves. My ensemble screamed *boss* and *sexy* at the same time.

"Good, 'cause I'm so excited." Mercedes stood up, and she was rocking a long-sleeve, fitted dress that gripped her assets as well.

"Me too." After setting the alarm, I locked Sierra in and we were on our way.

For this special occasion we opted out of driving and reserved a Cadillac Escalade with our very own personal driver. This night was special to me. We fought hard to get where we were, and we deserved it. The fast and dangerous life was over, and we were legit business owners.

The driver opened the car door for us and helped us climb inside. "Good evening, ladies. My name is Felipe, and I will be your driver for the night. I have the directions in my GPS, and your estimated arrival time is 32 minutes."

"Nice to meet you," Mercedes smiled and extended her hand.

"The pleasure is all mine," he smiled back, exposing a dimple in his left cheek. Felipe grabbed her hand and kissed it before letting it go.

"Nice to meet you, Felipe."

"It's my pleasure to be in the presence of such beautiful ladies."

"Woo, he got taste." Mercedes laughed while Felipe helped us into the truck and closed the door. "You like black girls, Felipe?"

"I've never dated one before, but I have seen some very beautiful ones, like tonight."

"Thank you."

"You're very welcome."

Mercedes sat by the window and I was by the door. Felipe shut us in and went to the driver's seat.

On the way to the club the ride was very smooth. There was no traffic, and surprisingly 95 south, didn't have any construction going on. I swear every time I came this way lanes were always blocked off. The universe was really on our side tonight, so I knew everything would be perfect. The only thing missing was Corey.

"B, did you ever think we would get this far?" Mercedes was looking out the window, taking in the view.

"I knew we would do it. There was never a doubt in my mind." I paused to keep myself from tearing up and ruining my makeup. "I just never thought it would only be the two of us."

"I know, right?" Mercedes sniffled. "I know they're looking down at us, smiling."

"Yeah, they are."

Felipe pulled up in front of the club, and the line was wrapped around the corner. My heart fluttered with excitement. Our dream had finally become a reality. Felipe opened the door and let us out.

"Feel free to come inside, 'cause it's going to be a long night," I told him.

"Okay, thank you. Just in case you don't see me in there, I'll be outside waiting on you."

"Okay." We strutted through the doors feeling like celebrities.

After having a 30-minute meeting with the staff, we were ready to open the doors for business. Every supporter outside the door was let in, one-by-one. The DJ was on the ones and twos, spinning the latest Rick Ross joint, and the waitresses were walking around taking drink orders. I had to say I was impressed with the crowd standing before me. Mercedes and I sat back and waited for the doors to close before making an announcement.

Standing by the DJ booth, he passed me the mic and cut the music.

"Hello, everyone. I just want to say thank you for coming out to Chyna's Dolls. We greatly appreciate it. On your way in you were given a ticket, and that is for a free drink of your choice. A lot if you know me, and some of you don't. Original-ly, there were 4 of us who started this business, and now it's only the two of us because the others were taken too soon, which makes tonight bittersweet."

Thinking back to the day we thought of this made me choke up and freeze, losing my words. I was still in disbelief. Mercedes saw I was struggling and took the mic.

"Sorry, it's still hard for us because it's so fresh, but we want everyone to have a good time and turn the fuck up. Let's get lit in this bitch," she shouted.

Mercedes passed the mic back to the DJ and grabbed me by the hand. "Hey, we agreed there would be no tears shed to-night. We are going to mingle and have a little fun. After it's over, we'll have us a drink on the way home until we pass out."

"Okay. I can be so sensitive." I managed to chuckle a little bit.

"Only when you love someone," she laughed. "Let's go have some fun shit."

I was game for that, so I followed as she led the way.

For the next hour I mingled amongst the crowd, stopping to talk to the people I knew from the hood. Amon was also in the building.

"This shit lit, cuz." Amon hugged my neck. "I'm proud of you."

"Thanks, cuz. I appreciate that."

"Corey told me to tell you 'congratulations.'"

"Yeah, he could've called me and told me on his own. It's cool, though."

"This was hard for him to do, but he had to in order to get his self together. Us men," he patted his chest, "we love hard. And when we get hurt, it's like the end of the world. It may seem selfish, but it is what it is."

"Yeah, I see that." I frowned. What he was saying may have made sense to men, but it was crushing a bitch's heart.

Love should be stronger than pride.

Just when I was about to verbalize that thought to Amon, I saw his eyes widen with surprise, and he was staring over my shoulder.

Oh my god! My heart skipped several beats. I didn't have to turn around to know who he was staring at. It had to be my boo. I just knew there was no way Corey would miss my grand opening, especially when he knew what I went through to make this happen. Him surprising me felt so romantic. This was going to be a perfect night after all.

Smiling, I slowly turned around to greet my king with a hug and kiss, but the person I encountered was not him!

What the fuck?

My arms froze in midair. A tall black man wearing all black with a shiny badge around his neck stared at me with contempt. My arms fell to my sides.

I cleared my throat. "Um. How can I help you?"

"My name is Detective Steve Rhines, and I'm looking for Barbee Kingston."

My perfectly-made eyebrows shifted downward. For the life of me, I couldn't understand what he wanted with me. Then it dawned on me something probably happened to Corey.

"I'm Barbee Kingston."

"Can you come with me for a second? I need to speak to you in private."

Amon stepped in. "Whatever you need to say to her can be said in front of me."

226

Detective Rhines reached behind his back and pulled out a pair of ghetto bracelets. "Barbee Kingston, you are under arrest for the murder and armed robbery of Antonio Shields. You have the right to remain silent. Anything you say can and will be used against you in the court of law."

While detective Rhines continued to read me my rights, everything around me went silent. He stepped behind me and placed the cuffs on my wrists.

"She didn't kill nobody! What the fuck you doing?" Amon shouted.

"You may wanna step back before I arrest you for obstruction of justice."

"Don't worry, B, I'll be down there." Amon frowned and shook his head in disbelief. "Don't say shit to they ass."

Everything around me was moving in slow motion as they escorted me through the crowd. I could feel the stares of the patrons burning a hole through my soul, standing around and staring at me curiously.

On the way out I caught a glimpse of a guy wearing a ball cap, but he had it pulled down low to cover his face. There was something about him that was familiar to me, but I brushed it off. My mind was focused on this crime I didn't commit.

The cop placed me into the backseat of his patrol car and closed the door.

"Take a good look at your club before we pull off," the detective mocked. "You'll be 100 years old before you see this muthafucka again."

I didn't bite the bait. *Fuck saying anything to this bastard!* I reminded myself. But I couldn't help fearing his words might come true.

I sat on the hard plastic seat in discomfort and watched the club get smaller and smaller as he drove me away. Had that bitch named Karma finally caught up to me? I had always heard bloody money was hard to wash your hands of. Now I feared that was about to come true.

But if the detective thought he was going to break Blacque Barbee, he had the wrong bitch.

To Be Continued...
The Fetti Girls 3
Coming Soon

Stay Connected with Us!

Text **LOCKDOWN** to 22828 to stay up-to-date with new releases, sneak peaks, contests and more…

Thank you!

Destiny Skai

Coming Soon from Lock Down Publications/Ca$h Presents

BOW DOWN TO MY GANGSTA

By **Ca$h & Jamaica**

TORN BETWEEN TWO

By **Coffee**

BLOOD OF A BOSS **IV**

By **Askari**

BRIDE OF A HUSTLA **III**

THE FETTI GIRLS **III**

By **Destiny Skai**

WHEN A GOOD GIRL GOES BAD **II**

By **Adrienne**

LOVE & CHASIN' PAPER **II**

By **Qay Crockett**

THE HEART OF A GANGSTA **II**

By **Jerry Jackson**

TO DIE IN VAIN **II**

By **ASAD**

LOYAL TO THE GAME **IV**

By **TJ & Jelissa**

A DOPEBOY'S PRAYER **II**

230

The Fetti Girls 2

By **Eddie "Wolf" Lee**

A HUSTLER'S DECEIT **III**

THE BOSS MAN'S DAUGHTERS **III**

BAE BELONGS TO ME **II**

By **Aryanna**

TRUE SAVAGE **II**

By **Chris Green**

RAISED AS A GOON **II**

By **Ghost**

231

Destiny Skai

By **TJ & Jelissa**

RAISED AS A GOON

By **Ghost**

PUSH IT TO THE LIMIT

By **Bre' Hayes**

BLOOD OF A BOSS **I II & III**

By **Askari**

THE STREETS BLEED MURDER **I, II & III**

THE HEART OF A GANGSTA

By **Jerry Jackson**

CUM FOR ME

CUM FOR ME 2

CUM FOR ME 3

An **LDP Erotica Collaboration**

BRIDE OF A HUSTLA **I & II**

By **Destiny Skai**

WHEN A GOOD GIRL GOES BAD

By **Adrienne**

A GANGSTER'S REVENGE **I II III & IV**

THE BOSS MAN'S DAUGHTERS

THE BOSS MAN'S DAUGHTERS II

A SAVAGE LOVE **I & II**

232

BAE BELONGS TO ME

A HUSTLER'S DECEIT I, II

By **Aryanna**

A KINGPIN'S AMBITON

A KINGPIN'S AMBITION **II**

By **Ambitious**

TRUE SAVAGE

By **Chris Green**

A DOPEBOY'S PRAYER

By **Eddie "Wolf" Lee**

WHAT ABOUT US **I & II**

NEVER LOVE AGAIN

THUG ADDICTION

By **Kim Kaye**

THE KING CARTEL **I, II & III**

By **Frank Gresham**

THESE NIGGAS AIN'T LOYAL **I, II & III**

By **Nikki Tee**

GANGSTA SHYT **I II &III**

By **CATO**

THE ULTIMATE BETRAYAL

By **Phoenix**

Destiny Skai

BOSS'N UP **I & II**

By **Royal Nicole**

I LOVE YOU TO DEATH

By Destiny J

I RIDE FOR MY HITTA

I STILL RIDE FOR MY HITTA

By **Misty Holt**

LOVE & CHASIN' PAPER

By **Qay Crockett**

TO DIE IN VAIN

By **ASAD**

234

BOOKS BY LDP'S CEO, CA$H
(CLICK TO PURCHASE)

TRUST IN NO MAN

TRUST IN NO MAN 2

TRUST IN NO MAN 3

BONDED BY BLOOD

SHORTY GOT A THUG

THUGS CRY

THUGS CRY 2

THUGS CRY 3

TRUST NO BITCH

TRUST NO BITCH 2

TRUST NO BITCH 3

TIL MY CASKET DROPS

RESTRAINING ORDER

RESTRAINING ORDER 2

IN LOVE WITH A CONVICT

Coming Soon

BONDED BY BLOOD 2

BOW DOWN TO MY GANGSTA

Destiny Skai